RAISED ON IT

A BETWEEN THE PINES NOVEL

LISA SHELBY

LISA SHELBY BOOKS, LLC

Raised On It
Copyright (C) 2020 Lisa Shelby Books, LLC
This book is a work of fiction. Names, characters, businesses, places, events, and incidents are either the products of the author's imagination or used in a fictitious manner.
Any resemblance to actual persons, living or dead, or actual events is purely coincidental. All rights reserved. This book or parts thereof may not be reproduced in any form, stored in any retrieval system, or transmitted in any form by any means—electronic, mechanical, photocopy, recording, or otherwise—without prior written permission of the publisher, except as provided by United States of America copyright law. Except for the original material written by the author, all songs, song titles, and lyrics mentioned in Raised On It are the property of the respective songwriters and copyright holders.
Cover Design: Bite Me Graphic Design
Editor: Jenny @ Editing4Indies

ALSO BY LISA SHELBY

The Between the Pines Series

(Meet *The Crew* from Eastlyn in this four book series of standalone contemporary romance novels.)

We Are Tonight

Raised On It

Bottle It Up – Preorder Now

Leave the Night On – Preorder Now

Blackbird

Standalone second chance contemporary romance.

The Gorgeous Duet

A steamy, suspenseful romance about breaking the rules and following your heart.

Gorgeous: Book One

Gorgeous: Book Two

The You & Me Series

Read this three-book series of sweet and sexy standalone novels filled with love, loss, secrets, and sass.

You & Me: Part One

You & Me: Part Two

More

Something Just Like This

S,

I'm so glad I've had you to sing along with all of these years.

As always, this is for you.

Sam Hunt and everyone involved in creating the songs that make up the, Between the Pines - Acoustic Mixtape album,

Thank you for the inspiration, the epic road trip sing a longs and all the feels.
Your little mixtape has been a part of the soundtrack of my life for years, not to mention the characters in this series.

~ L

Raised On It
(A Between the Pines Novel)

By
Lisa Shelby

CHAPTER 1

Miles

The Verdict.

There's something about this place. Always has been.

Maybe it's the glow of the neon light reflecting off the hardwoods of the beer-stained dance floor. It could be the ice-cold drinks or the artery-clogging fried foods, but I'm pretty sure it's the people.

Eastlyn, Oregon, and the people who live here are what connects me to the real world. What keeps me grounded.

Any time my head starts to hit the clouds, somebody in this town is sure to pull me back down to earth until my feet touch the soil again.

That being said, one particular Eastlyn resident is starting to get on my last nerve.

"Scheana, you've checked your lipstick ten times already. What in the world has gotten into you?"

"Be nice, Miles."

"I am being nice. You're a beautiful girl; you don't need any of that crap. You never have. So why are you so decked out for a night of karaoke at The V with me of all people?"

Charlie Myers is blasting us with his rendition of "The Thunder Rolls," just like he does every Saturday night, while Scheana and I wait our turn.

There isn't much to do here in Eastlyn, but you'll always find someone you know to share a beer with here at The Verdict. Also known as The V, this bar is somewhat the epicenter of Eastlyn. Where you go after a wedding shuts down and you want to keep the party going. Where you go for an ice-cold beer and the best cheeseburger in Eastern Oregon. It's where you go to dance your blues away, sing your heart out, and meet up with old friends when they ask out of the blue.

Scheana's mom and my mom were best friends. We grew up together, just a year apart in school, and spent years listening to our parents sing along to classic country music. This is why when we karaoke, our duets always start with "Islands in The Stream," in honor of our moms and end with the hip-hop classic "Dilemma," in honor of the great Nelly and Kelly Rowland. Sure, Scheana and I hooked up one time right after high school, but this isn't shocking, considering my reputation.

Except for the girls in "The Crew," there aren't really many women in Eastlyn my age who I haven't hooked up with.

What can I say? I am who I am.

Regardless, Scheana and I are nothing more than friends, and our inevitable one-time indiscretion was years ago and never affected our status as longtime family friends. Tonight, she's distracted, and the fact that her distraction centers around her looks has me concerned. Scheana has never been insecure about the way she looks because, frankly, she has never needed to worry. She's adorable, but seeing her long black hair curled within an inch of its life, her face painted like she's about to go on a stripper stage instead of the karaoke stage, and her anxiety about how she looks in all of this war paint are giving me reasons to worry something is off with her.

I'm just about to lean over to ask her what's up when she entwines her fingers with mine on one hand while her other hand leisurely starts caressing my leg.

Whoa!

"Uh, Scheana, whatcha doin?'"

"What?" she asks even more distracted than before. Her face is pointed in my direction but her eyes, her eyes are certainly not looking at me.

I stop her shaking hand on my lap when I place mine on top of hers. "Sweetie, you know I love you like family, but since when do we hold hands?"

Before she gets a chance to reply, I follow her gaze to see what has her acting so crazy, and the entire evening is explained in an instant. Standing at the bar with a collection of his fellow roughnecks is her ex Adam.

Sitting back in my seat, I give her that look a parent gives you when they've figured out a scheme you're trying to pull over on them.

"Scheana, did you know Adam was going to be here tonight?" I sound like her dad, but I can't help myself.

She bows her head in humiliation.

Lifting her chin with my index finger, I lift her sad eyes to mine, and her pain and desperation cut through me.

"I thought you guys ended things months ago?"

"We did."

"And if I remember correctly, he broke your heart?"

"He did, but…"

"No buts. He told you he wasn't ready to commit, so why would you want him back?"

"I know I seem pathetic, but we were together for five years, Miles. Five years! I ran into his sister the other day, and she said that he ended things after he lost his job because he didn't feel he was good enough for me. It turns out, it wasn't that he couldn't commit to me, but he just wanted me to have more. Well, I don't want more, Miles. I just want him."

Oh, you sweet girl. Suze better not be messing with you.

"So if you want him back, why do you want him to see you with your hands all over me?"

Again, she doesn't need to say a word, her eyes say it all.

"Let me guess…if he sees you with a man-whore like me, his protective instincts will kick in, and he'll do whatever it takes to get you away from me before I get you in my bed?"

The blush from her embarrassment is deepening with every word that comes out of my mouth.

"Why, you little vixen, I do believe you're using me for my unsavory reputation with the ladies." I bring my hand to my chest and feign my disbelief.

"Oh, my gosh. I am so sorry, Miles…" Her eyes glisten, and she gets up and rushes to the bathroom.

Shit. I didn't mean to make her cry. I was just giving her a hard time.

Adam's a good dude. He may go from one roughneck job to the next, but he's not an asshole. I can't say the same for some of his friends, but Adam is a decent guy. And he's noticed us. He watched her rush to the bathroom, and he's trying his best not to storm over here and tell me to keep my hands to myself. It's pretty clear he's still crazy about her. It must be real because I've never seen a man watch a woman walk away like he was watching her. You can see the longing as well as the misery on his face from across the bar.

Damn, the asshole really does still love her.

Well, if she wants to put on a show, then we'll put on a show.

Mission: Get Her Man Back is in full effect.

"Miles, will you take me home please? I'm sorry I thought this was a good idea," Scheana says once she's gathered herself and returned from the ladies' room with a fresh coat of paint on her lips.

"Oh, sweetheart, we ain't goin' anywhere. He can't take his eyes off you, and we're gonna show him just what he's missing."

Swinging her out in front of me and then twirling her back into my arms, I two-step my way with her to the dance floor, and we proceed to dance our asses off for the next thirty minutes. We pass on "Islands in the Stream" this go round and sing "My Boo" instead when our names are called for karaoke. This seems to be the last straw because I can see Adam's jaw clenching from the stage.

When the song ends, I excuse myself and pretend I have to use the facilities, but what I'm really doing is giving him an opening. If he knows what's good for him, he'll take it, and if she knows what she's doing, she'll leave with me and let him stew for the night.

After wasting what I hope is sufficient time in the john, I make my way back to the dance floor only to find the two of them slow dancing.

That's what I'm talking about.

I know at the moment she's going to want to kill me, but I also know what I'm doing, and it's the right thing to do if she really wants to get him back.

Tapping on Adam's shoulder, I clear my throat. "Excuse me, but I think I'd like to cut in and dance with my date if you don't mind?"

Her eyes are pleading with me not to interrupt their moment while his warn me that if I'm not careful, he may just try to kick my ass.

He can try, but it will never happen.

"Sorry, Adam, but I'm a firm believer in that whole dance with the one you brought. So if you don't mind, I'll finish this song up with the one you let get away." I wink in Scheana's direction, and she catches on.

She takes a step away from him, and he turns around dejected. He heads back to the bar, leaving me to fill the space he's left behind.

"I know you probably want to kill me right now, but trust me on this one, okay?"

She nods.

"What did he say?"

"That he missed me."

Kissing her on the forehead, I whisper. "Good. He'll be yours again by morning."

"You think so?"

"Yep, we're gonna finish this song, and then we're gonna walk out of here together. You'll have a text waiting for you when you wake up."

We're making our last trip around the hardwoods when the bar door opens, and the music, neon lights, and all of the people filling the space around me fade away.

She's the most beautiful woman I've ever seen.

She's not from Eastlyn, this I know for certain.

If she were from Eastlyn, she'd be mine.

I know this body and soul.

Yes, she's tall, blond, and beautiful, but there is something more filling the atmosphere. I have no idea what it is exactly, but for some reason, I feel like the trajectory of my life has just completely changed.

"Miles, the song is over. Let's go."

No, no, no, no! Not now!

"Right, time to go."

Shit. Here's hoping I can take Scheana home and get back here before my mystery woman is gone.

Scheana puts her hand in mine, and we walk across the dance floor for the entire bar to see. Making sure everyone sees us leaving together.

Shit! Why now?!

My mystery woman takes a seat at the bar, and when she does, she takes a look around, clearly feeling like a fish out of water and trying to get the lay of the land. As her eyes peruse her surroundings, our eyes connect for the briefest of moments. Her cheeks turn pink, and even with the distance between us, I see something flash in her eyes, but when she looks down at my hand holding Scheana's, she immediately looks away.

We leave the bar and jump in my blue Dodge parked across the street, and I can't start the diesel engine fast enough.

"Do you really think this is going to work? He looked pretty pissed."

Knowing how insane I feel over possibly not meeting the stranger who just walked into my hometown bar, I can't even imagine how tortured Adam has been for the last hour.

"It'll all work out, Scheana. He'll see the light."

"God, I hope you're right. Why do I get the feeling this is going to backfire?"

"Nah, I know men, and you're it for him."

She falls silent, and in two minutes, we're parked in front of her place.

Always the gentleman, I get out and run around to open the door for her. I may be a man-whore, but it doesn't mean I wasn't raised right. She hops out of the truck, but I swear she takes the steps to her front door in slow motion. Either that, or I'm ridiculously anxious to get my ass back to the bar.

Once she's finally up the five—yes, I counted them in my desperation—stairs that lead to her front porch, I'm ready to watch her walk through the front door and listen to her lock it behind her so I can bail, but by the way she's bouncing on the balls of her feet and looking at me like Puss in Boots with those big eyes of hers, she has something to say.

"Miles, thanks for tonight. I really appreciate it."

Taking the keys out of her hands, I unlock her front door,

hoping she'll get the hint. "No problem, darlin'. Keep me posted, okay?"

Not budging, she speaks again. "I will."

"Okay, well you sleep well and lock up. I want to hear that deadbolt." I kiss her on the cheek and back up until I'm on the top step.

"Miles, did you get an invite to Brittany and Jason's wedding?"

"I sure did."

"Do you have a date yet?"

Shit.

"Uh, hadn't even thought about it yet. I just opened the invite a couple of days ago."

"Wanna go together? I just can't imagine going alone if Adam's there too. It won't be a date or anything."

"Sweetie, you two will be back together by then, and you won't need a plus one, but if for some reason that isn't the case, then of course I'll take you. Now go get some sleep and stop worrying about everything."

Finally stepping across the threshold, she says over her shoulder, "Thank you so much, for everything." Then ever so slowly, she smiles and waves and thank Christ finally shuts and locks the deadbolt.

I'm down her front steps in a flash and flipping a bitch in the middle of her street to get my truck headed back in the direction of the magnetic woman I'm pretty sure just changed everything.

My truck feels like she's driving through mud, and the two-minute drive feels like it's taking forever.

A voice from within that I've only heard on a couple of different occasions is shouting at me to get back to the damn bar, and when I finally push open the bar door and find her laughing at what must have been one of Beau's legendary bad jokes, my heart starts working overtime. I swear I can feel the blood thumping through all four chambers of my heart at once.

Goddammit, she finally found me.

CHAPTER 2

Mason

So far so good.

Katie was right. Everyone in Eastlyn has been incredibly friendly, and the local bar is just as she described it.

Much bigger than it appears from the outside and full of life, the bar has booths that line the walls and a long L-shaped bar on the far side. There's a dance floor that has seen better days but supplies plenty of room for dancing in front of the tiny stage where a cute little redhead is currently belting out her version of "Firework" and doing a pretty good job of it. There are a couple of small tables and chairs near the stage as well.

There are cowboy hats, baseball caps, and bald domes adorning the heads of young twentysomethings and older locals. All the women in the bar are the epitome of the girl next door no matter their shape or their size. It's like the small-town version of Cheers where everybody knows your name.

Beau, the bartender, introduced himself and asked where I

was from, not even bothering to pretend there was a chance I was local. He was friendly but not intrusive.

More importantly, he knows how to pour the perfect pint of my favorite lager.

Katie gave me a pretty good rundown on the local cast of characters. I have a list of names in the notes on my phone, each with a little comment of things I need to know about them. I know I'm supposed to stay away from the creepy bar guy, James. If he makes a move, I've been instructed to get Beau's attention, and he'll take care of it with a look.

Other than possibly falling into bed with the town playboy, she said I should be fine. What was his name again? Hot, sandy hair, charming, farm boy, but what was his dang name?

Oh well, I have no intention of falling for the town hottie. Been there, done that. Well, not a small-town hottie but the playboy of the Upper East Side.

They're all the same.

I have no intention of going down that road again.

Beau places my order in front of me, and the drool I feel begin to form in the corner of my mouth is clearly an indication of how hungry I am. I had no idea until the food was in front of me, but suddenly, I'm ravenous.

"One Verdict burger, no mayo, no onion with a side of tots. Ranch and ketchup are on the plate, need anything else?"

"I'm all set. Katie said it was the best burger in town, and after a day of traveling, I'm starving. I have a feeling this is just what I need."

"Katie? Do you mean Katie Sandoval? Are you the house swap gal?"

"That would be me," I reply, wondering if I should stop sharing so much with a total stranger.

"Of course you are! I forgot you were showing up this week. Katie told me to look after you and to make sure to keep James away from you. He creeps the girls out and has been known to cause a scene."

"She warned me about him, thanks." I giggle.

"Well, I got you, girl. Promised Katie I'd look after you. We're all real proud of our Katie girl. Happy to see her following her dreams and getting her big break. You need anything, just let me know."

"She's a sweet girl, and I think the timing was perfect for both of us. The only thing about swapping homes with her is that I won't get to see her on stage. I have a feeling this is just the beginning for her, though. I'm sure I'll get my chance to see her another time."

"Well, all of us here in Eastlyn are glad she's got a safe place to stay while she's in the Big Apple. Thanks for setting her up. Again, you need anything at all, just holler."

"Thanks, I'll be sure to hold you to that. Now, let's see what this burger is all about."

Beau throws his bar towel over his shoulder and crosses his arms in front of his Verdict T-shirt-covered chest and waits for me to take my first bite of the giant burger. I sure hope this is as good as he thinks it's going to be. He's pretty confident.

Squishing the bun as small as I can, I take my first bite, barely fitting it in my mouth. I do believe I have just taken a bite of burger perfection. Beau is right to be confident. It's delicious.

I moan around my mouth full of food, unable to speak, but words aren't necessary. Beau knows exactly what I would say if I could, and he gives me a *that's what I thought* nod and walks away.

I can't help but giggle at his gesture. I really think I'm going to like this place if this first meal is any indication.

When I think about where I was yesterday and where I am sitting right now, I can't help but think this may have been the craziest thing I've ever done.

I met Katie at a party just a week ago, and here I am, sitting on a barstool in small-town Oregon while Katie is most likely asleep in my Manhattan apartment overlooking Central Park.

When the two of us hit it off at Lala's party where we were celebrating the new cast of what will hopefully be the next Broadway smash *The Lights*, everything just happened. She had been telling me about her hometown of Eastlyn, the town that also happens to be the home of my favorite beer, and when I said it sounded like the perfect inspiration for the new small-town series I was writing, she said I should come stay at her place while she's in New York for the next three months.

When I realized she wasn't joking, I asked her where she was going to be staying. She said she hadn't worked it out just yet, and this gave me the idea. I suggested she stay in my apartment, and I go to Eastlyn. This way, she'd be comfortable and safe in the city, and I'd have the perfect reason to escape everyone and everything and hopefully find some inspiration along the way.

It took five minutes to figure out, and a week later, here we are.

When I first got to town, I thought for sure I had made a mistake. I was surprised and a bit shell-shocked. Katie told me it was a small town, but I had no idea just how small it was. I mean Main Street is just that, the main street in town. There is only one stoplight, and the focal point of the town is the courthouse and the big white church at the end of town.

Katie's house is small but incredibly cozy. I thought I had known what shabby chic was, but I really never had any idea until I opened the front door to Katie's place. It's feminine and comfortable, just what I need. I felt inspired instantly.

Then I walked into this place, and the doubt crept back in.

It's one thing to be alone in Katie's adorable house but another to be out amongst the locals where I'm the only person who doesn't know somebody else in the room. Fortunately, Beau and my Verdict burger have me feeling back at ease.

Besides, it's too late now.

I'm here, and Katie's there.

This is happening.

I wash down my last bite with the last of my beer and pop a tot in my mouth. When was the last time I had a tater tot? I can't help but feel I've missed out on so much by not having them in my life regularly.

Burger. Beer. Tots. Ranch dressing. Does it get much better?

"Another beer?" Beau offers when he sees I've drained the golden deliciousness that once filled my pint glass.

"I shouldn't."

I can hear my wishy-washy tone before Beau lifts an eyebrow in question because he knows I really want to say yes.

"Fine, yes. One more but only one!"

"Nobody's twisting your arm, honey."

"Gah, I know! I just can't believe I'm sitting in Eastlyn drinking EBC. Dreams really do come true." I laugh.

Alternating between ranch and ketchup, I continue eating my tots at a leisurely pace. The karaoke is off, and the house music is playing classic 90's country and I can't help but turn around on my stool to check the place out some more.

When I do, I'm hit square in the chest with that *what have I done* feeling again. Tables full of friends talk and laugh, and when I catch the eye of a table full of women who look to be my age, I can't help but feel as though they aren't happy to see a stranger—make that a female stranger—in their bar.

I can't turn around quickly enough and am resigned to the fact that if I keep my back to everyone, I won't be reminded just how out of my element I am. But I try to remind myself that this is the first night, and I'm here to write, not to make friends. At least I have Beau on my side already. I guess I've made a friend, after all.

Still, I think I'll throw this next pint back quickly and get the hell out of here and head back to the comfort of Sycamore Lane where everything is throw pillows and all things cozy.

Out of nowhere, I'm covered in goose bumps when a feeling comes over me that I can't explain. Something that says don't ask for the check just yet.

"I'm going to marry you one day," a deep voice says from the barstool next to me.

What the hell?

"Excuse me?" I say, staring at the baseball game on the TV above the bar. I couldn't care less about baseball, but with what his voice did to my body, I'm scared to death to face the person attached to it.

"I knew it the moment you walked in."

Is this guy for real?

"Wow, does that pickup line really work?" I reply, still without looking at him.

I'm such a chicken.

"Nah. I don't really need to use pickup lines in these parts."

"Who are you?" I ask the TV.

"Miles Montgomery at your service. What can I get you?" His voice is like butter, and I'm melting on the spot with every word he speaks.

My brain is yelling at me to get a grip, but my lady parts are finding it hard to fight his charm and silky-smooth voice.

Oh, this is not good. I can feel it.

Wait.

Miles Montgomery.

His name is on my list as one to watch out for.

Shit.

Knowing I need to proceed with caution, I slowly twist my head in the direction of the deep baritone voice that came from what was once the empty stool to the right of me.

Sandy hair. Check.

Caramel eyes full of trouble. Check.

Bronzed skin that says my days are spent outside and I'm probably a farm boy. Check.

A smile that could disintegrate a fragile pair of lace panties without even trying. Check.

The obvious charm Katie warned me about. Check.

Dangerous to my heart. Without a doubt. Check. Check. Check.

When he tilts his head just so and hits me with a casually sexy smile, my mouth hangs open as if my jaw has fallen off its hinges, bewildered by the mere presence of the man.

The words I had planned to put together letting him know I wasn't interested float away like the dust particles illuminated by the neon on the walls. Leaving me looking like an idiot.

As his smile grows, the heat I feel on my cheeks burns hotter.

Get it together, woman. He's just a man, nothing more.

Get. A. Grip.

"No thanks, already have one on the way. Along with my check." I say that last part a little louder so Beau hears me. I take a glance in the bartender's direction to make sure he heard me and to get my eyes off the man next to me.

Beau shoots me a wink, and I watch him fill my pint with care refusing to look back at the Greek god next to me.

"Go ahead and close your tab. I'll take it from here."

Wow, Katie wasn't kidding. He's already living up to his reputation. At least his arrogant attitude will make it easier to resist his charm.

Choosing not to look at him when I reply, I instead stare at the same baseball game I couldn't care less about. Feels safer that way.

"Thank you, but I'm fine. Don't need you to take anything from here."

"Consider me the welcome wagon. I know everyone in this town, and I don't know you. I think we need to change that."

"Nah, I think we'll both be fine if we don't."

"Come on now, don't be that way."

Beau interrupts and saves me from having to reply.

"One EBC and the check. The burger is on me. Welcome to town."

"Thank you, but you don't need to do that."

"I know, but considering you have to drink your beer with this idiot bugging you, it's the least I can do."

I giggle another thank you and take a sip of the ice-cold perfection in front of me.

"I thought we were friends, Beau. Don't do me like that," Miles says from his barstool.

"You want anything, asshole?" Beau says with obvious affection. These two clearly know each other well, and I can't help but play along with their playful banter.

"So, Beau, you seem to know Mr. Montgomery well. On a scale of one to ten, one being a virginal Boy Scout and ten being a psycho killer, where would you rate this guy?" I still don't look in the farm boy's direction, simply aiming my thumb toward him.

"The truth?" Beau questions.

"Nothing but," I reply firmly.

Beau throws a glance at Miles before the prematurely salt and pepper bartender replies. "I'd trust him with my life but not my sister."

His answer hits me in the gut. Of course he's a good guy. He just can't keep it in his pants.

"Is that right?" I question Beau but finally get the guts to face the man in question.

He just shakes his head and whispers, "Don't believe a word he says. Well, except the good parts." He makes a motion that says Beau is crazy and then gives me a wink, only his wink does something to me that the others I've gotten from my new friend behind the bar haven't.

His wink gets me all hot and bothered, and I guzzle half my pint in the hopes it will cool me down.

It doesn't.

"Listen, he's good people—" Beau elaborates but is quickly interrupted by the topic of conversation.

"You know, I'm sitting right here, right?"

Beau ignores him and continues. "As I was saying, our boy here is good people, the best actually. Just hang on to your panties because he'll be in them before you know what hit ya."

A peanut hits Beau between the eyes. He picks it up and throws it right back to where it came from.

"You're just envious of my devilishly handsome good looks. I can't help that I was born with the face of an angel. We all have our lot in life."

"Oh, please. I saw those devil horns peeking out the moment you said hello. I've seen your type before. Big cities…small towns…they all have them," I chime in.

"Them?" He looks at me confused, but I know his game.

"Those charming playboys we all know better than to fall for. The kind your family always falls in love with but are always too good to be true. I know your type all too well, Mr. Montgomery."

"Miles. Please call me Miles."

"Damn, she's got your number already. I think I'll leave you to dig yourself out of this one all on your own. Nice to meet you and let me know if you need anything at all. You know where to find me," Beau says leaving me to school Miles on my own.

"So, if I'm the charming playboy, then who are you?"

"I'm the girl who thinks she's different than the rest. The one who'll be able to change you, but I think we all know how that story ends."

"So cynical."

"Nah, just wise. Trying to learn from my mistakes instead of repeating them over and over again."

Chugging back the rest of my beer, I make a show of slamming the glass onto the bar and then standing. "So good."

"You like EBC, do ya?"

"It's my favorite. It's hard to find on tap on the East Coast. I'm gonna get spoiled."

"How long are you here?"

Taking my purse off the little hook under the bar—the hook all bars should be required to have—I throw it over my shoulder, ready to take my leave and simply ignore his question.

"I didn't catch your name," he says.

"That's because I didn't give it to you."

"What brings you to Eastlyn?"

Go! Don't answer him, just go!

I'm trying to be cool. You know, ice in the veins and all that, but something in those eyes of his warms me right to my core and turns my insides to goo. God, he's good. My mouth starts explaining how Katie and I met and how we came about switching houses.

"Just like that movie. So, are you Kate Winslet or Cameron Diaz?"

"Ha-ha! Katie and I said the same thing. We both love that movie, but I'm surprised you've seen it. I didn't take you for a rom-com kind of guy."

"Darlin', there's a lot you don't know about me." He says this like this fact is going to change. "So, you're a writer? That's really cool. Did you always know you wanted to be a writer?"

Without giving it a second thought, I sit back down on my stool and tell him about what a voracious reader I was as a child and how much I loved my creative writing classes in school. I tell him about my intentions to self-publish while working a day job, but before I even got the opportunity, I met the right person who became my agent and got me a book deal right out of the gate. I'm one of the lucky few whose first book sold well, and after ten books in the same series, it's time to start something new.

"Wow, we've got a celebrity in our midst."

"Hardly. I use a pen name. Nobody knows who I really am."

"Well, if you need a tour guide to show you all the ins and

outs of our little town here I'd be more than happy to slap on a name tag and be that guy."

"Thank you, but I think I'll manage."

"Let me walk you home. I know Katie's place is on the other side of town."

"I'm just parked outside, but thanks." He's holding my gaze so fiercely the warmth I felt from his wink is now warming me all the way to my nether regions, and his ridiculous start to our conversation is all but forgotten.

Or so I thought.

"Okay, well have a good night, and I'll see you soon."

My eyes roll on their own volition, but he doesn't quit.

"What? How are we going to plan the wedding if we don't get to know each other?"

Oh.

My.

God.

This man is insane, and I'm speechless.

Turning on my heels, I speed walk across the bar, fleeing like a frightened animal. Pulling the door open, I'm screaming at myself not to do it, but of course, I look back, and just as I thought they would be, his eyes are still trained on me.

He yells at me from across the bar. "I'm in your head. You won't be able to stop thinking about me now." I can see his perfect white teeth shining through his Cheshire cat grin all the way over here.

I am in so much trouble.

CHAPTER 3

Miles

It's only nine, and it's already pretty clear I'm going to be nothing but a waste of space here today.

I'm distracted.

Twitchy.

I'm in my head yet not able to think a coherent thought to save my life.

"Peter, I'm gonna head to town. Be back later."

"Sounds good. Still don't know why you insist on coming in every day. I know it's harvest, but we're all good here, boss man."

"Nice try. I can't even imagine what kind of debauchery would happen if I didn't keep you on your toes."

He shouts something back at me, but I've slammed the truck door before actually hearing what he says.

He's right. I don't really do any of the real work around here anymore. Hell, I don't even do any of the paperwork now that I have a full-time accountant, but this place is my home. My heart and soul are seared deep into the soil of this farm, and I can't imagine my life without it in it. It's what I've done since I was a kid working for my granddad.

Today, I showed up as the sun came up, but I didn't do shit. Not much has gotten done since I looked into those dark brown eyes on Saturday night. Eyes she tried to keep from meeting mine, but when they did, I saw everything in them. From a fiery strength to a warm softness, those eyes have had me a complete and utter mess since.

Add to that everything we have going on with the business and I am useless.

Might as well drive into town and get some coffee. Sure, I have a thermos full of the stuff that I made at home this morning, but I need a distraction. Well, at least a different distraction. One that will pull my head out of my ass.

Besides, Brass Tacks has the best coffee in Eastern Oregon and is owned by one of my best friend's sisters, so there's always a pretty good chance for some sort of conversation popping up that could eat up a nice chunk of my time.

As if the universe has decided to jump on the Team Miles train, there's an open spot smack dab in front of the coffee shop. Not that this is a bustling city but parking on Main Street in front of a local favorite like Brass Tacks is rare on a Monday morning.

When I push open the door, the bell hanging above chimes as it always does, but the static in the air is all new. I know instantly the distraction I've been trying to get away from is right here in the coffee shop I'd hoped to escape in.

I've barely moved my head to my right, and the damn ground below me sways slightly when the vision that is my mystery woman comes into sight. She's tucked away in one of the overstuffed brown leather chairs in the back corner, hair up in a high ponytail, face naturally fresh with barely an ounce of makeup, and with her casual jeans and T-shirt look, this woman is a wonder.

I know she said she's from the East Coast, but I can't imagine a woman as divine as her could be from anywhere other than the heavens above. I'm not a religious man, but I'm thanking the big guy upstairs for putting this heavenly creature in my path.

"Miles! What are you doing over there?"

Becks' voice gets my attention, and I force myself to tear my eyes away from the angel in the corner and to the face behind the counter looking at me in a way that says *what the hell is wrong with you.*

Looks like I took two steps in the door and stopped in place and have been standing here staring at the new girl in town like a stalker. Luckily, she has earbuds in, and she didn't hear my name called, and I'm able to reach the counter without being detected.

"Hey, Becks, how's it going?"

Becks is family. My girl, Amelia, was a bit of a surprise to her parents, and Rebecca, or Becks as we all call her, her big sister, was almost ten when she was born. She may not have been an official part of *The Crew,* but she was a big sister to us all. She's the stable one—married, two kids, running her own business and still taking care of anyone who needs her. Don't even get me started on her famous cheesecake. She's kind of like a superhero to all of us. Not only *can* she do it all but she *does*.

"I'm good. Not distracted like some other people who think it's good for business to stand still with his giant body blocking the doorway so nobody else can get in." Her head nods in the direction of the blond beauty in the corner.

"Can you blame me? I mean, look at her, Becks. Have you ever seen anything like her before?"

Becks is five foot three if she's lucky, so she has to hop up a little to lift herself up on to the counter to lean forward and place her hand on my forehead.

"Dude, what are you doing?"

"Checking to make sure you aren't ailing from a fever of some sort." Her hand moves to my cheek. "You feel fine. Strange. Does this mean an alien has taken over your body?" She pretends to look all over my face. "Miles, are you in there?" She drops back down to her feet.

"Smart-ass isn't becoming on you, Becks."

"Sorry, I've just never seen you so taken by a woman before."

"I know, it's crazy, but the moment I saw her at the bar the other night, she had me out of my head."

"No shit?" she whispers, looking as though she's seen a ghost or something.

"Don't be so shocked. Just because I get laid often doesn't mean there isn't still a heart beating in this extremely toned chest."

"You are ridiculous. You want your usual?" she asks, exasperated.

All it takes is one of my egotistical comments to right the world again and have her focused back on why I'm really here.

Caffeine.

All I get is a black coffee so it only takes a minute for my cup to be poured, but I use every second of that time to watch her, and it's the most entertaining minute of my life.

Mystery woman has her laptop fittingly on her lap and is so engrossed in what she's reading she doesn't seem to realize she's destroying the straw in her iced coffee with the way she's gnawing on it. A few seconds later, she releases the straw and takes a sip. This simple action has me getting a semi right here in the morning light with a crowd around me.

Damn, this woman.

She lifts her cup to take another drink, but something on the screen has her smiling and silently giggling. Once the giggle stops, she brings the straw close to her lips that are now sitting slightly parted and her lower lip is screaming for me to bite it.

Finally, her chewed within an inch of its life straw makes it between her perfect pink lips.

Victory!

"Here's your coffee, dummy."

"What?"

"If she notices you staring at her, you're just gonna creep her out. Take it down a notch, psycho."

"You're right. I'm goin' in."

"Not at all what I meant. Oh, the poor girl."

Slowly, I approach as though she's a wild bunny who might hop away if I get too close, too fast. She puts her cup on the table in front of her and there it is, her name.

Mason.

Not what I expected, but I like it. It fits her.

Taking the seat across from her, I don't say a word as I wait for her to notice my presence. And when she does, it was more than worth the wait. When she sees it's me, her dark eyes light up, and her lips start to curve upward, but then she stops herself, putting her armor in place.

A challenge. I like it.

Pulling out her earbuds, she looks at me but waits for me to speak.

The hours of recalling her face didn't do her justice.

I stare back.

It looks as though we have a good old-fashioned standoff going on. Not how I usually make my move, but there isn't anything usual happening here.

I guess the game goes on a little too long for her liking because she starts to put her earbuds back in, ready to ignore me, but I do win in the end because she speaks first.

"Nice to see you too, Miles."

"Whatcha up to, Mason?"

"How did you…?"

Nodding to her cup where her name is scribbled in black marker, I answer her question before she gets it out.

"Well played."

Instead of putting her earbuds in, she untwists the cord nervously.

"So are you writing about the charming local stud you met at The Verdict the other night? Or are you already writing about the wedding day?"

"You are so stupid."

My intelligence is being questioned for the second time this morning, and it's still early. Damn.

"You kinda like it, though, don't you?" I reply.

"If that's what you need to tell yourself."

"It will happen, Mason. There are forces in the universe that cannot be explained and, more importantly, cannot be denied. There isn't anything either one of us can do about it."

"What are you doing here this time of day on a Monday? Unemployed?"

She ignores my declaration. That's fine. I'll give her a break for now.

"Nope. Been at the farm since sunup. It's just a few miles out of town. Thought I would take a little break."

"Oh, that's cool."

"So, Mason, why did you leave New York City for our humble little town? I can't believe it's solely for book inspiration."

"I just needed a change of pace and yes, a little bit of inspiration."

"Seems like there are a lot of places you could have gone for inspiration."

"Sure, but Eastlyn is just what I needed. My next series is going to be set in a small town, and I can't think of a better place to find my muse."

"Is that right?"

Her eyes roll, and she shakes her head, but she does laugh.

I'll take that as success.

"The *town* is the muse I was looking for."

"Whatever you need to tell yourself."

"Ugh. But seriously, when I met Katie, things just fell into place, and it's as though it was meant to be. I already love it here. Everyone is so welcoming. The weather is a little warmer than I expected, but I think this is gonna be a great few months."

"Well, my offer still stands if you're looking for a tour guide."

Unlike the first time I asked her, she doesn't say no right away. I can tell she's thinking it over by the way she chews on her bottom lip. Damn, she's hotter than hell.

"Thanks again. It's really nice of you to offer, but I think I'll be okay."

Rejected once again.

"Well, if you change your mind, just let me know."

She nods and puts her earbuds back in, effectively ending our conversation.

She sits back in her chair, and when she realizes I'm not leaving simply because she's dismissed me, she lifts her eyes and one eyebrow, asking what I'm still doing here.

We're locked in on each other, neither of us wanting the moment to end, even if only one of us will admit it. When I see that sparkle light up her deep brown eyes again, I know this isn't over.

She'll change her mind.

Maybe not today, but eventually.

She knows it too.

She's just not ready yet.

I'll wait.

CHAPTER 4

Mason

"Katie, your place is just great. I cannot tell you how much I love it here. Thank you so much for trusting me to stay in your home."

"Uh, what are you talking about? I would trade my tiny little house to live in your Manhattan skyrise any day! Your apartment is amazing. Thank you so much for agreeing to our little house swap!"

"Let's just agree that both of our places are great, just different. I have a feeling I'll be making some interior design changes once I get home. I had no clue that I needed more shabby chic throw pillows and blankets in my life, but I. So. Do!"

"Right? A girl can never have too many soft things. So, have you met many people yet?"

"As a matter of fact, I have."

"Oh, do tell."

"Well, Saturday night, I went to The Verdict, and you weren't kidding, their burger is amazing!"

"Told you!"

"You were also right about Beau. He was really nice and made sure I knew he was there if I needed him."

"Yep, he's a great guy. If you need anything at all, he'll be there. So, who else?"

"Well, that guy Miles Montgomery you warned me about…"

"No way, on your first night!"

"Yes, on my first night but don't worry, he didn't even get my name, at least not until this morning when I saw him at Brass Tacks."

I purposely leave out the little fact that I'm apparently going to be marrying him one day.

"Oh, I miss Brass Tacks already. New York is great, but they haven't perfected their coffee game, that's for sure. Tell Becks I said hi the next time you're in there. Now, let's get back to Miles. How in the world did playboy extraordinaire Miles Montgomery not score your name? I can't imagine how crazy it must have made him!"

"I just didn't give it to him. We talked, and he tried. He really did. Even offered to be my tour guide while I'm here, but for some reason, it felt right not to give him my name. He's kind of fun to mess with."

"That he is, and from what I hear, in more ways than one. So what did he do to finally get you to cave?"

"I didn't cave, but I also didn't have my guard up. He cleverly found it on my coffee cup when he sat down at my table."

"Oh, snap! He foiled your flirty little plan."

"I wasn't flirting. It was just too much fun to string him along for a little bit. Besides, I know his type, and I have no intentions of falling prey to his dastardly ways."

"Oh, come on, who knows what you might be missing, right? Miles may be a player, but he is also a ton of fun. You're only there for three months, so why not enjoy yourself? If you go in knowing he's not the love of your life and he's just temporary, then Miles Montgomery is the perfect way to fill your time."

"But he was on your list! You told me if anyone was going to try to get in my panties, it would be him. Now you're saying I should let him in?"

"Well, I didn't think you would meet him on night one, and that you would have such a great time toying with his emotions. I think you might just be what the big guy needs to be put in check."

"I don't want to put him in check, Katie."

"Yes, you do. Besides, nobody loves Eastlyn more than Miles. If you really want inspiration from our small little town, there is no one better to guide you."

"Katie…I don't know."

"I do. Just say yes. Have a little fun. It's not forever; it's just for now. Do it!"

"Well, who knows if I'll even see him again. I may have already missed my chance. Now, tell me all about opening night!"

Changing the subject is a must because I cannot talk about the hot farmer in the tight-fitting jeans anymore. He isn't for me, and temporary fun or no fun, I cannot let myself fall for another man-whore.

Another charmer.

Another man who will say anything to have his way.

It's something I refuse to do.

CHAPTER 5

Miles

Katie Sandoval is my new favorite person.

When I got her text asking me if I could go over to her place and fix the stair on her back deck, I couldn't help but kiss my phone. Especially when she ended the conversation with "good luck."

She knows more than she's letting on, and my guess is that she talked to her house guest and my name came up.

Damn skippy, if that doesn't feel good! If doing some manual labor for Katie is what it takes to get Mason to notice me, then by all means, let me do her this favor.

As if Katie's house was on fire instead of having a loose board on her deck, I rev up the engine to my truck, and Lou and I haul ass to town.

In ten minutes flat, we're pulling up to the curb outside her place.

I waste no time, taking the front porch steps three at a time. I knock on the door and wait.

And wait.

And wait.

My excitement begins to fade when I realize she may not be home. I wonder if she's at Brass Tacks? Would I look like a stalker if I went there to find her?

I'm about to turn away when the click of the deadbolt sends my heart racing, and when the door swings open, you could knock me over with a goddamn feather. Her hair is piled on top of her head in a messy bun, and she's wearing a white T-shirt that says, "Romance Writers Do It Better" on top of a pair of loose boxer shorts.

Well, fuck me running. There isn't a breath left in my lungs.

In the two seconds I was able to take a quick inventory of her, I'm already hotter than the steaming cup of coffee she's holding in her hands.

Where did this woman come from?

"First, the coffee shop and now, you're here at my front door. Will mine be your first restraining order, or is there a list as long as my arm?"

"Darlin', you may look sweet enough to put in my Rice Krispies, but I'm not actually here for you."

I'm such a liar.

"You really are something, aren't you?" she says, not flinching at my remarks.

She's a tough cookie, and I love the game we're playing. Eventually, our little game will soften her up, and I plan on finally taking a bite.

"Mason, you have no idea."

Her eye roll has my dick twitching. This is by far the best morning I've had in recent memory.

"So why are you here exactly?"

"You're looking at your local handyman. Katie texted me and asked me to fix the broken boards on her back steps. I can show you the texts if you need proof?"

Leaning against the doorframe, she doesn't reply, but she does set her unrelenting gaze on me. She's contemplating whether to believe me. The whole scenario does seem a bit suspicious, but at least I have the backup to prove I was actually summoned here. I would be more than happy to sit here and stare at her all day, but as much as it pains me to admit, she's kicking my ass at the moment with her stare down. The fact that she isn't budging is a little unnerving.

"Well, I'm just gonna go around back and get to work. Oh, and I'm gonna have my pup with me, so if you see a German shepherd running around the backyard, he's with me."

Not able to stand the blank expression and lack of words coming from her, I leave her on the porch and make my way back to the truck to get my toolbox from the back and my boy out of the cab. When I turn around, she's gone, and I'm disappointed.

* * *

IT'S ELEVEN THIRTY, and the board is fixed. As are many other boards that looked like they could possibly become loose in the next five years. I've mowed the front and backyard, and I've thrown the ball for Lou.

Now, even I have to admit I'm starting to look a little desperate or, at the very least, obvious as I dejectedly gather my tools. I'm just about to call Lou over so we can head out when the unmistakable squeak of a screen door opening stops me in my tracks.

"I'd say you did more than fix a loose board."

Rendered speechless, all I can do is shrug at the beauty standing in front of me, her long floral dress blowing in the breeze.

"Thanks for mowing. I appreciate it."

"I figured I was here so…"

She smiles. I mean, she really smiles. And everything is off balance. I feel like an insecure middle schooler about to have his first kiss.

Saving the day Sweet Lou bounds through the yard and rushes the porch and Mason. Panic ensues, and I reach out, trying to stop him before he jumps all over her.

"Whoa, buddy! No!"

"It's okay, isn't it, big guy? Come see me."

She doesn't shy away from my ninety-pound ball of fur. No, she pats her legs and eggs him on until he pulls loose from my grip on his collar. I only let him go because I know he wouldn't hurt a fly. Where most people are cautious around a strange German shepherd they've never met, Mason has no reservations. She squats down and isn't just petting my dog, she's hugging him while he licks her face.

And just like that, I'm jealous of my dog.

"Hi, sweetheart, what's your name?"

"Mason, meet Lou."

"Hi, Lou. It's nice to meet you, buddy." She spots his ball next to her foot and throws it for him.

Smart girl.

Wiping the dog fur off her dress, she stands. "He's sweet."

"Sweet Lou, that's what I call him."

"It fits. He's adorable."

Lou is back and drops the ball at her feet. She bends down to get the ball and then pretends to whisper in his ear.

"Does your daddy ever work?"

"Uh, what do you call what I was doing for the past three hours?" I ask incredulously at her insinuation.

She throws the ball again but doesn't reply.

"Hey, have you been to The Jury Room yet?"

"I can't say that I have."

"Well, you haven't really been to Eastlyn if you haven't been to The Jury Room. How about you let me take you to lunch to say sorry for Lou's behavior."

"Hmm…"

"What do you say?"

"Sure, what the heck."

That's what I'm talking about!

Bless you, Katie Sandoval.

"I'm all done here, so if you're ready, I'm ready. I'll just take Lou to the truck and meet you out front."

"Sure. I just need to put on some shoes, and I'm ready to go. Meet you out there."

Lou and I head around the side of the house to make our way to the truck, both of us with a little extra spring in our step.

"I knew you'd like her, buddy. She's pretty cool, isn't she?"

He barks in agreement when I let him in the crew cab of the truck, and then I hop in the front to get the engine started and the air conditioning pumping while I wait for her.

When she floats through the front door, I can't get out of the truck fast enough to get the passenger side door open for her. She glides down the front steps, and her honey blond hair is blowing on a breeze I can't even feel.

"Milady."

I make an effort of escorting her into the truck, and she's so distracted giving my so-called man's best friend scratches behind the ear that I'm pretty sure my display goes unnoticed. I shut the door and make my way around to the driver's side of the truck in shock. I am legitimately jealous of my dog.

I'd let her scratch me behind the ears if she wanted.

"You aren't going to leave this sweet boy in the truck while we eat, are you? It's already getting pretty warm."

She's a dog person. I think she might just be perfect.

"Nah, you don't need to worry about Lou. He'll be just fine."

"Good. I hate to think of you as one of those awful humans who leaves their dogs in a hot car in the middle of summer."

"Well, once you get to know me a little better, you'll know that would never be me."

"Is that so?"

"Yes, ma'am."

"Hmm…"

She spends the rest of the short drive quiet, looking out the window and thinking God only knows what.

When we pull up to a nice shady spot near The Jury Room, the diner sitting directly across the street from the courthouse, she hops out before I can get her door so I let Lou out of the cab and grab his bowl and a bottle of water. I let down the tailgate so he can jump in, fill his water bowl, and throw him the treat I had tucked away in my pocket.

Mason is waiting for me on the sidewalk, and the look on her face says she's impressed with my relationship with my dog. I'm glad it matters to her. I don't think I could be in a relationship with a woman who didn't care about my dog, and a relationship is what I'm going to have with Mason O'Brien.

Even if she doesn't know it yet.

Even if I've never really been in one before.

"How's my handsome boy?" The sweet local florist whose shop, Busy Bee's Flowers, is next door to the diner says, wasting no time coming out to greet my dog, but not me.

"He's good, Mrs. Thoms, but what am I, chopped liver?"

"Oh, Miles, if only you were as sweet as your pup."

She gives me a wink but puts her hand out to Mason.

"And who do we have here?"

"Mrs. Thoms, meet my friend, Mason. She's staying in Katie's place while she's in New York taking over Broadway. I thought I'd take her to lunch since she hasn't been to the The Jury Room yet."

"Hi there, it's nice to meet you," Mason says, shaking hands with the sweet Mrs. Thoms. "I was just admiring your display. It's gorgeous," Mason compliments the front window of the flower shop with sincerity.

"Oh, I like you already. You swing by anytime, and I'll be sure to make you something pretty. Now, don't let me keep you. You two enjoy your lunch and make sure you leave room for a slice of pie. You won't regret it. And you better make him pay. Lord knows he can afford it."

Did she really just say that?

Nobody in this town has any scruples, I swear.

We say our goodbyes and snag a booth with a window and a view of Lou so I can keep my eye on him. Not that I need to. He's so doted on by everyone in town, it's ridiculous. By the time we order our meal, three different people have already stopped by to show him love.

"He seems to be a bit of a local celebrity. But so does his daddy."

"Nah, it's all about Sweet Lou. I'm just his driver. I bring him to the people, and he eats it up. He's an attention whore, that one."

"Why do I get the feeling you're a bit of an attention whore yourself?"

She can lift that pretty little eyebrow all she wants; I have no shame in my game.

"I know what people say about me, and I can't imagine what people have probably told you. The thing is, it's all true, but I'm still the most trustworthy guy you'll meet."

"Hmm. You are, are you?"

"Damn straight. I'm as faithful as they come. I may be loud, and like my dog, I may be a bit of an attention whore. I will never deny that I'm a flirt, but I have never cheated on anyone."

"From what I hear, you've broken many hearts."

"I can't help it if women have more feelings for me than I have for them, but it doesn't mean I have ever promised more than I was willing to give."

"And why is it you aren't willing to give them more? Do you come from divorced parents, or was your heart broken when you were younger?"

Well, looky there. She's trying to figure me out.

She is sure going to be disappointed.

"Nope, my parents have been married for thirty-eight years. They are the happiest, most in love couple I have ever seen. Don't even get me started on my grandparents. It's because of the four of them that I never promise more than I can give."

The little crease between her eyebrows is a clear indication that she's trying to read into my answer. Dissecting me inside that pretty little head of hers.

"Mason, I know what it looks like to be with the one you were meant to be with. My parents are the perfect example of what we should all strive for in a relationship. I haven't met my person yet. Have never been lucky enough to fall in love. I'm a patient man, but I can't wait for her to finally show up."

The sun shining through the window highlights the rosy glow spreading across her cheeks. Her mouth hangs open for a beat before she catches herself and closes it.

Clearly, she wasn't expecting my answer.

"You've never been in love?"

"I can't say that I have."

But I have a feeling my luck may be changing.

"So that girl I saw all over you the other night knows you aren't gonna put a ring on it?"

"Scheana was actually using me to get her ex's attention."

"I'm sorry. What?" She chokes on her Cherry Coke.

"Yep, she loves Adam in a big way, and he loves her right back. In fact, when I came back to the bar to talk to you, he stopped me at the door ready to fight for her. I made sure to let him know what she was up to, and if he was smart, he'd go get his girl. They were back together by morning."

"Wait, did you say you came back to the bar to talk to me?"

There's no stopping the smug smile forming on my face because in my book, I just won this round. All that talk of true love between Scheana and Adam and all she heard was the part about me coming back to the bar to talk to her.

"You heard me right. I dropped Scheana off at home and was so desperate to get back to the bar before you left that I even agreed to be her date to a wedding in a few weeks, and I don't take dates to weddings."

"Gotta leave your options open?"

"Listen, you never know when a bridesmaid is gonna drink too much champagne and need a ride home. I'm a damn Boy Scout, I tell ya. Wait until you meet the girls in The Crew. They'll set you straight."

"The Crew?"

"That's what my closest group of friends and I named ourselves back in middle school. There are seven of us, eight if you count Parker's wife, Audrey, and we're like a little family. If you want to know anything about me, the good, the bad, or the ugly, just talk to The Crew, and they'll fill you in. We may not all live in Eastlyn anymore, but we're still just as close."

"That's really cool."

"It is. I'm a pretty lucky guy. So what's your story?"

"I don't really have one."

"Sure, you do. You said you've known plenty of men like me, so there has to be a story there. Oh, and you're wrong about that, by the way. You've never met anyone like me."

"There you go. You two need anything else?" our waitress, Sherry, asks when she drops off our food.

"I'm good, thanks," Mason replies with another sincere smile.

"How about you, sweetheart?" Sherry asks, turning her attention my way.

"I'm good, but I'd love it if you'd answer a question for me?"

She's suspicious, but she bites. "What question is that?"

"Have you ever met anyone else like me, Sherry?"

Her head falls back, and the belly laugh that follows answers my question.

"Oh, darlin'..." She has to catch her breath after her moment of hysterics. "I certainly have not. Miles Montgomery, you are one of a kind, to say the very least."

"Told you," I say to the smiling beauty across the table from me.

"Oh, sweet girl. You've met your match with this one. He could charm the skin off a snake. Don't say you haven't been warned."

After a giggle, Mason replies. "Thanks for the warning. I'll keep that in mind."

"Sherry, you're really never gonna leave Stan and run away with me, are you?"

As always, Sherry shakes her head and walks away after my playful flirting. She always pretends I exhaust her, but she loves every second.

As soon as it's just the two of us again, the first thing Mason does is sneak a fry off my plate.

"Hey, if you wanted fries, you should have ordered them," I say, scolding her, but deep down, I'm crazy glad she's comfortable enough to eat off my plate.

"I don't want a bunch, just a few. Besides, how are you gonna stay in that kind of shape if you eat all these fries? I'm doing you a favor." She winks. "You're welcome."

So you have been checking me out.

Did I just win round two?

Suddenly, she's relaxed and flirty. It's pretty damn sexy.

"I'll share my fries, but it's your turn to share."

Actually, I'd let her eat everything on my plate if it kept her in this playful mood, but I really do want to get to know her.

"There isn't much to tell." She shrugs and fills her mouth with her ranch-covered chef salad.

"Nice try. Somebody did something to you. You don't get this cynical if you haven't been screwed over. Besides, I want to hear about all these guys you've met who you claim are just like me."

She finishes her bite and takes a sip of her soda.

"Well, we won't even go into my college sweetheart who it turns out wasn't just the life of the party but was also just using me for sex. I thought we were in love, and he was just into getting laid on a regular basis. But the one who really did the damage was Grant. I was with Grant for nearly five years. He was handsome and charming and said all the right things."

She lifts an eyebrow, which I am learning is something that makes my dick twitch, even if she is using the move to be a smart-ass.

What can I say? It's hot.

She's hot.

I might need to invest in some loose-fitting sweats or shorts or something if this dick twitching is going to become a thing.

As much as the dick twitching is distracting, I'm not missing a word and committing everything she's sharing to memory.

"He too was a flirt. Young and old, there was no discriminating. Men, women, gay, straight, he was the person who made everyone feel good. The life of the party. He came from a good family, went to the best schools, and had a great job. I too came from a good family and went to good schools, so on paper, we were a perfect fit. Except, in the end, he hated my job." She looks me dead in the eye the entire time she speaks. Making sure I hear every word.

Don't worry, sweetheart, I'm hanging off every syllable.

"What didn't he like about your writing?"

"Apparently, writing romance isn't classy enough for the likes of him."

"Sounds like he was afraid he couldn't hold a candle to the

men you write about. See, there's another thing I don't have in common with him."

After another dramatic eye roll, she continues. "If that weren't enough, we were at a party at my parents' house when I caught him screwing a needy little socialite on my dad's pool table. When I confronted him, he couldn't figure out what my problem was. Turns out, he didn't really believe in monogamy. It also turns out he was only with me for my family name, connections, and of course the family money."

What a fucking idiot.

"Mason, I'm real sorry this Grant asshole couldn't see what he had and chose to hurt you like that."

"To top it all off, when I went crying to my girlfriends, they weren't surprised in the least. Seems I was the only one unaware of his constant indiscretions."

"Your friends knew and didn't tell you?"

"They knew all along. Even when I gave up my apartment in the city to move to the burbs with him. I worked so hard to afford that apartment and buy it on my own. Not my family's money, but my own. I started writing a column for a women's magazine in college, and when my first series hit it big, I saved every penny and had enough for my apartment before my books became a TV series."

"Whoa, Mason. That's awesome. Congratulations on all of your success. So, we really do have a celebrity writer in our midst."

"Thank you, but I'm not a celebrity by any means. If only I hadn't given up so much of what I had worked so hard for, for him. For the man I thought I was going to marry one day. If only it hadn't been for a man who was sleeping with most of the Upper East Side and using me as his arm candy. However, that was three years ago. Now, I have an apartment overlooking Central Park again, and I'm back where I want to be."

"Good for you."

"I learned a lot about myself and what I'm not willing to give up in the future."

What I wouldn't do to meet Grant one day. To tell him what a colossal fuckhead he is to not only waste a life with a woman like Mason but also to beat his ass for hurting her so badly.

Dick.

CHAPTER 6

Mason

I've been walking around with my head in the clouds since Miles's truck drove away from Katie's place after our spur-of-the-moment lunch. I've been so distracted that I completely spaced about my nail appointment and jumped out of my skin when my phone pinged, reminding me I was supposed to be at the salon.

I am never late for anything.

Well, at least I wasn't until I met Miles Montgomery.

Luckily, Tell Me About It is smack dab in the middle of Main Street, so I don't have to think too hard to get there because my mind is all over the place.

If someone had told me when I woke up this morning that I would be having lunch with Miles, I would have laughed in their face. But watching him try to come up with things to do outside to delay leaving was not only obvious but also quite endearing. He wasn't trying to get my attention, but I couldn't help but sneak peeks out the kitchen window and maybe even the bedroom window.

I love New York City, but no penthouse, no matter how big the mortgage, has a view as good as the one I had this morning looking out into that backyard.

Central Park is nice, but the landscape here comes complete with backward baseball caps, sexy work boots worn from years of work and weather, and denim that fits in a way I didn't know was even a thing.

The best view in town is one that has both Miles and Lou in it.

Yes, watching his tan, toned arms flex while he worked did a little something to me, but watching him with his dog is why I went to lunch with him.

I was kicking myself all the way to The Jury Room, but once we got there, our conversation flowed easily, and shockingly, I told him about Grant. Not only did he find my career and my success interesting, but he asked question after question. And the best part? His inquisitiveness seemed entirely genuine.

Now, here I am, running late and feeling as confused as Lou was when Miles would pretend to throw his ball only he couldn't find it anywhere because it was still in his dad's hand.

That's exactly how I feel right now.

Everything about the man should have me running in the other direction. He might as well have a big red circle with a line through it on his chest.

But then there all those other attributes he has with his charming ways that most men don't.

He listens. Like really listens.

He isn't threatened by my success.

He wants to know the way my brain works and about my writing process.

He wants to know what makes me tick.

But the jaded part of me can't help but think all of this could just be the way he thinks he can get in my pants?

Will the other side of him, the side of him he hasn't shown me yet, come out once he gets what he wants?

I park Katie's Honda in front of the salon and silently thank God that I'll finally have something to do to take my mind off Miles.

The salon is adorable, adorned in pink and red lips that go with the theme of the name out front. There are several employees as well as two clients, and I can't help but feel as if I've interrupted their conversation when the room falls silent and all eyes are on me as I approach the front desk.

"Welcome to Tell Me About It. You must be Mason?"

"That's me. I have an appointment with Cara for a mani/pedi. I'm so sorry I'm late."

"Nice to meet you. I'm Cara and don't give it a second thought. We're gonna sit right over here in the open chair. These are my friends Emmett and Amelia, and they were just telling us about their crazy trip to Vegas. They were there during the big blackout last week."

Both women say hello and welcome me. I haven't met a person I didn't like in Eastlyn. I have a feeling it's gonna be hard to leave this place.

Hating to interrupt, I urge them to continue their storytelling and the petite redhead Cara introduced as Amelia continues her story.

"So as I said, we weren't just in Vegas during a blackout, but we were with Nicolette Gwen when it happened. And I don't mean she was across the room or in the building. We were backstage! In. Her. Dressing. Room!"

"How in the world did you end up in the same dressing room as Nicolette Gwen?" Cara asks the question we're all thinking while she removes the old polish from my toes.

"This one arranged it," she says, aiming a painted thumb in Emmett's direction.

I'm pretty sure that was her name. She looks so familiar to me, like really familiar. Only I cannot figure out why. Tall, thin, and with a head full of foil. "Emmett and Josh are besties with 'Nikki' as Em calls her."

Cara and her co-workers squeal and fangirl over Emmett and start asking questions about what the famous pop star is really like. Emmett answers a few questions but graciously steers the conversation back to Amelia.

"Honestly, you guys, it was a little scary. Not only did the lights and power go out but there was also no cell service. Twelve hours with no cell service had some people ready to blow a gasket. Not to mention, Reece and Rachel were stuck in an elevator. Twelve hours did the two of them plenty of good, and now they're back together, she's going to Africa with him, and all is right in the world. He even delayed going back right away so he could fly back with her. They leave in two weeks."

"Aw, it's good to hear the two of them are back together after all these years. It's nice to know second chances really do exist," the woman doing Emmett's hair says. "But tell me, who freaked out the most? Was it you, Amelia?"

"I would have thought so too, but it wasn't our sweet Melly. It was actually the one and only Josh West who started to have a minor meltdown. You would have thought his phone was keeping him alive, and without it, he might just die on the spot. I think he might even be a little afraid of the dark. But if you tell him I said that, I'll deny it."

The moment Emmett says the name Josh West, I know exactly why she looks familiar. She's dating the biggest movie star on the planet, Josh West. I've seen her all over the tabloids the past couple of weeks.

Eastlyn, Oregon, keeps getting more and more interesting.

"Josh didn't freak out for long, though," Amelia, apparently also known as Melly, chimes in. "Miles did what Miles does and calmed him down."

"I bet he tried to calm Nicolette Gwen down too," Cara says, confirming it's my Miles she's talking about.

My Miles?

What in the world is wrong with you? He is far from yours, Mason. You don't want him anyway. Remember?

"Nah, Miles was too concerned with making sure our entire Crew was okay to worry about Nicolette. He's who kept us all calm. He would go get information and updates from the hotel staff, and of course he kept us all laughing." Amelia backs her friend up, describing the Miles I've gotten to know and not the version Cara referred to.

"Once he finds the right girl, Miles is going to make one lucky lady very happy. This I know for sure."

"Emmett, I couldn't agree with you more," says the stylist whose name I can't remember.

Hearing them talk about Miles this way has my heart giddy-upping on the inside, and my skin blushing on the outside.

They have no idea the stranger who has infiltrated their chat fest was just at lunch with the topic of conversation a mere hour ago. Nor do they know how I desperately hope not to let him under my skin, but I can already feel the itch from him finding its way just below the surface.

"It's too bad nobody here at home has ever been more than a good time to him. I know we call him a man-whore, and I mean, I guess he is, but he's never cheated on anyone. He's just never settled down with anyone. You can't cheat if you don't commit, right?"

"Well, he may be a man-whore, but he's our man-whore," Amelia proudly claims Miles as one of their own from under the pile of foil wrapped hair hanging in her face.

"Once he meets her, he'll be a goner, and I think he's gonna surprise the judgy folks in this town. Enough about us. Tell us about yourself, Mason," Emmett says from the chair next to me.

All heads turn in my direction. "I'm sure listening to us talk about people who are total strangers to you is boring as hell."

Honestly, I could listen to you talk about Miles all day but...

I fill them in on how I met Katie and why I'm here. Where I've eaten so far and how I like the town. But I neglect to mention that apparently, I'm going to marry Miles Montgomery.

Five minutes later, Amelia and Emmett are inviting me to meet them at The Verdict for drinks later tonight and I'm accepting.

Just like that.

Since when do I say yes to lunches with hot men I have no business spending time with and drinks with complete strangers I just met in a salon?

Eastlyn is doing something to me, and so far, I think I like it.

CHAPTER 7

Miles

I hit send on my phone, sending a message to Amelia that says I'm still coming but running late.

Lou stares at me from the front window as I pull away from the house, guilt-tripping me in the process. How do people leave their kids at home? I can barely leave my damn dog home alone.

It's a short drive to town, and I'm a little surprised to see how busy Main Street is for a weeknight. Should be a fun time since Reece is home and a good distraction from thinking about the doe-eyed beauty who will only be a few blocks down the road. Luckily, I had a Skype meeting with the team in Portland to occupy my time this afternoon, but those eyes are always haunting me.

The moment I pull the heavy wooden door open—before I've even had my first glimpse of neon—I know she's here. Goddammit if I don't feel a change in the atmosphere, like a crackle, when she's around. What's more surprising than feeling her in the room is finding her on the dance floor with my best friends.

I'm not trying to be a creeper, that title already belongs to Chris, Emmett's ex who's staring at her from the bar, but watching her sing and dance along with Amelia, Rachel and Emmett has taken me by surprise and doesn't compute in my brain.

She's shaking her hips with her hands above her head, one holding a bottle of EBC.

I think I just might be in love.

Wanting her is one thing but seeing her effortlessly meld so well with my friends like this is a whole other story.

There's something about her that's a little more refined than the rest of us. She doesn't act differently, but deep down, it's there. This isn't her normal, and she's enjoying getting to live like the rest of us regular folk for a change.

Thinking it's time to stop stalking her like a pervert over here in the corner, I take my first step toward the bar when I see Peter, my lead at the farm, step up behind her and start bumping and grinding. I wouldn't say I'm seeing red, but I know for certain I don't like what I see.

Not giving it a second thought, I hastily make my way to the middle of the dance floor just as Mason turns around to see who's all over her ass.

Mason's eyes are as big as saucers when she sees me approaching.

That's right, honey. If you're dancing with anyone, it will be me.

I tap Peter on the shoulder and give a simple shake of my head letting him know the new girl in town is off-limits. Without question, he walks off the dance floor.

"Oh, really?" she yells over the blaring music, full of sass.

"Really."

"Who says you have a say in who I dance with?" This time, she pops up on her tiptoes so she can talk in my ear.

"I do," I say back in hers.

Gotta say, I love being this close to her.

"Is that so?"

"Does a cat have an ass?"

"What in the...?" Her head falls back on her shoulders in uncontrollable laughter, and I do believe she's more than fine with me stepping in. "Did you just ask me if a cat has an ass?"

"I did. And does it?"

"Yes, of course!"

"Well, there you have it. That's how certain I am that I have a say in who you dance with."

"You. Are. A. Crazy. Person."

"I think you like it. I think you like me."

"Insufferable! That's what you are!"

Before I can reply, we're interrupted by Emmett and Amelia, looking a little irritated.

Amelia takes the lead. "So you two know each other?"

"We met my first night in town." Mason seems embarrassed to admit.

"Of course you did," Emmett says, smacking me on the arm. "We thought she was *our* new friend, but of course she already met the unofficial Eastlyn welcome wagon."

"Hardly. I've offered to give her a tour of town, and she keeps shutting me down."

"Hey, I let you take me to lunch today!" Mason counters.

"Wait, so you had been to lunch together before we met you at the salon today?"

Mason bites her lower lip nodding her head.

"So, when you heard us talking about Miles, you knew who we were talking about?"

"I figured it out," my favorite little romance writer sheepishly admits, but what she's admitting, I have no idea.

"What are you guys talking about? Why does Mason look like the cat who ate the canary?" I yell over the music.

"Oh, no reason," Emmett says, not giving me even an inkling about what they're talking about. "Who needs a beer?"

"Me!" The other girls yell in unison, effectively ending the conversation and leaving the dance floor.

On Amelia's way off the dance floor, she mouths, "Sorry," while Mason grins from ear to ear. As she passes by, I let my fingers lightly graze hers, and much to my surprise, her fingers start to entwine with mine. But the moment is fleeting because as soon as she does, she lets go. When the tips of her fingers glide across the palm of my hand, I feel currents of electricity shooting through my entire body.

If this is what her touch does to me here in a public setting, then I'm afraid we might just burn this town down if we were to ever take this to the sheets.

Not that I'm in any kind of rush. This woman is the real deal, and I have no intention of messing things up, which is why I seize the moment before her hand has completely left mine, lifting it above her head and twirling her in a circle in front of me.

My man, Chris Stapleton, does me a solid and starts to sing a slow tune made for cuddling up real close on the dance floor.

"Dance with me."

She doesn't have to answer with words. The squeeze of her hand, and the bite of her lip along with the sparkle in her eye and the crackle in the air tell me she would like nothing more.

When I twirl her out in front of me—only to bring her back against my chest—her hands instantly find my shoulders, and she says, "Hi." I know she's right where she wants to be.

"I see you were so desperate to get to know me that you befriended my Crew."

"If that's what you need to tell yourself, then you go right ahead. I just happened to meet them at the salon today, and we hit it off. Besides, you don't seem too unhappy to see me here."

"Happier than a puppy with two peters."

Our slow sway is interrupted by her laughter.

"First, a cat's ass and now, a puppy's peters. Do you have some strange inappropriate fascination with domesticated animals?"

"If it keeps that smile on your face, I sure do."

Once again, her eyes light up.

It's crazy how good it feels to make her smile.

"I really like your friends."

"Me too."

"They're a part of The Crew you were telling me about?"

"They sure are. They're my family. I'd do anything for them."

"And you've never dated any of them?"

"Somebody sounds a little jealous."

"Not jealous, just curious."

"Well, you can tuck that little green monster of yours away. They've always been like sisters to me."

"Cool."

We look like we're at prom with the way her hands are around my neck and my hands wrap around her waist. I'm afraid to change our position, though. I don't want to scare her away, so prom it is.

The song is over way too soon. The legendary George Strait comes on, and I start right in on a leisurely two-step before she can even think about her escape.

"Whoa, what are we doing? I have no idea how to do this."

"It's easy. Follow my lead and just remember it's quick, quick, slow, slow," I explain as I take the steps.

She instantly looks down at her feet.

"Eyes up."

Her head pops up as instructed, and those soulful eyes of hers are wide and full of life.

"There you go. Just look at me and trust I have you."

"Miles, I feel like such an idiot." She loses the rhythm, and our feet collide. "You make it sound so simple."

"It is. Say it with me. Quick, quick, slow, slow. You can feel it."

"Quick, quick, slow, slow. Quick, quick, slow, slow. I think I feel it." Her face is determined, and there's an adorable little crease between her eyebrows. She's focused, and giving this her full attention.

Her eyes stay locked with mine as we both chant, "Quick, quick, slow, slow," together until the crease between her eyebrows is gone, and her focused look is replaced by pure joy.

"Whoo-hoo! I've got it!" she yells, celebrating her victory.

"Oh, yeah?"

I twirl her out in front of me, and she squeals, but when she comes back to me, I haven't missed a step, and she falls right back into it with me.

"Oh my, God! I'm still doing it! I've really got it, even after you tried to mess me up with your complicated little spin or whatever that was!"

"You must have had a good teacher."

This earns me one of her eye rolls.

"I think we work well together, don't you?"

Another eye roll and a shake of her head but her beaming smile says she's having fun and agrees with me. She doesn't have to admit it. I know we're good together and so does she. She'll get there.

I hear my name being yelled from across the bar and find the girls holding up fresh bottles of beer and pointing at the table they've procured for the evening.

"Shall we?"

Leaving the crowded dance floor is the last thing I want to do, but I don't want to push my luck either. If I keep Mason all to myself, I'll never hear the end of it.

* * *

CHECKING MY WATCH, I can't believe two hours have passed since we joined the other girls and Reece. Two hours of beers, laughter, and currently a crazy-ass game of Never Have I Ever. It certainly has been an educational way to get to know Mason a little better.

"You've seriously never had sex outside?" Rachel questions Mason in disbelief.

"I grew up in a crowded city. What can I say? I'm sure people have sex in Central Park all the time, but not this girl."

Of course my mind is racing with all the different places in the great outdoors I'd like to use to change her answer for the next time she plays this game.

"Well, I guess there are more benefits to being a country girl than I knew. Your turn," Rachel replies, turning the game over to Mason.

"Okay, let's see... Never have I ever had a threesome."

All eyes are on me, waiting for me to drink, and when I don't, they turn suspicious.

"I call bullshit!" Reece proclaims. "What about that time you left the Round Up with those two girls from Pendleton?"

"Nope. In the end, the blondee wasn't into it. Besides, the redhead was more than enough on that occasion. I've come close but no threesomes here."

I hear Amelia in the background calling me gross, but my attention is directed to the person who asked the question. At first, she was glad to hear I hadn't had a threesome, but I don't think she enjoyed hearing me talk about being with the redhead, and that feels all kinds of good.

A couple of girls we went to high school with show up as does Amelia's boyfriend, Andrew, putting an end to the game but giving me the chance to take Mason for another swing around the dance floor. We two-step, cha-cha, and slow dance.

There isn't a lot of talking besides my instructions on the steps to each of the different dances, but the silence isn't awkward.

The touch of our hands and the closeness of our bodies say more than any words could.

The crackle of electricity that runs between us is undeniable.

The bar is thinning out, which means the night will soon be ending. If I had my way, Beau would lock the place up and turn out all the lights, and I'd stay right here slow dancing with her in my arms.

I swear my friends are out to get me. It's like they can't help but ruin the moment and make sure I don't get my way when they interrupt us to say their goodbyes.

"Mason, you walked here, didn't you? Did you want a ride?" Amelia asks since she was the DD for the evening.

"Thanks for the offer, but after all of that beer, it'll do me some good to walk."

"Don't worry, I'll walk her home."

Three heads swing in my direction and Amelia, Rachel, and Emmett couldn't be more obvious with their reactions, and Andrew can't fight his smile. They think I plan on getting in Mason's pants.

"Relax, I'll be a perfect gentleman." I pop my arm out, and thankfully, Mason takes it.

We walk right out the door, leaving the three troublemakers without another word.

Mason's laughing again. It sounds better than any of the country classics we heard tonight.

Like on the dance floor, we don't talk much as we walk through town, but with the darkness of the night blanketing us, it's a comfortable silence.

Once Katie's house is in view, I rack my brain for something gentlemanly I can do to prolong the evening but only come up with ideas I am sure she would consider far from appropriate.

"I'm really glad Amelia told me to meet them at the bar tonight," I say, breaking our silence.

"Me too, Miles. I had a lot of fun."

She takes the steps up the front porch. I can't help but follow her like a needy puppy. Once she's on the porch, she stops and turns to me. Standing one step down from her, I am at her eye level.

We both know what we want to happen next, but I'm not sure she's ready.

"Mason, is it okay if I k—"

Before I can finish my question, she fists my shirt in her hands, pulling me closer so her lips can find mine. Her kiss is soft, yet intentional and has me a bit stunned. But as soon as I get over the fact Mason made the first move, I take her face in my hands and kiss her back. Our tongues dance, and the heat between us is palpable, but the pace stays slow and meaningful.

This is it.

This is what I've waited thirty years to feel.

This is why I haven't committed to anyone before her.

This right here is what it's all about.

Too soon for my liking, she gently pushes away, but her hands are still wound up in my shirt, and her face is still in my hands. She may be stopping the kiss she initiated, but all it does is give me the opportunity to get a front row view to the seductive eyes that have been keeping me up at night.

"Spend the day with me tomorrow," I blurt out, not giving it a second thought.

I need more.

She takes in a big breath, letting go of my shirt and smoothing it out with her hands. Taking a full step back, she effectively breaks our connection when she says, "Thank you for the invite, but I don't think that would be a good idea."

"Why not?"

"I need to get back to what I came here for, and that's my writing. I really need to spend the day working."

She's full of shit.

She's scared because she feels it too.

She knows she's gonna fall hard if she isn't careful.

"Let me see your phone."

There's no hiding the skepticism on her face.

"I just want to give you my number in case you change your mind or you need your lawn mowed."

There goes the eye roll I'm starting to live for.

"Sorry, that sounded bad, but you know what I meant."

She pulls her phone out of her back pocket, unlocks it and hands it to me. She's biting her lip again. I've already figured out this is something she does when she's feeling shy, and knowing I do that to her feels good as long as she doesn't shy away from me in the process.

I program my number into her contacts but pause before hitting send on a text to myself, so I have her number too.

"You okay with me sending myself a text so I have your number too?"

Biting her lower lip a little harder, she nods her approval still looking shy.

I hit send.

My front pocket chimes, and I hand her back her phone.

Walking backward until she reaches the door, she says, "Thanks for walking me home. I'll see you around I'm sure."

Isn't she cute, thinking she'll see me around. Like this would ever be it for us?

"I'll wait here until you're inside."

"Oh, um…okay."

She digs her key out of her front pocket, and I realize she isn't carrying a purse. And for some reason this really turns me on.

She turns and fumbles with the lock but eventually gets the door open.

"Night."

"Sweet dreams, Mason."

CHAPTER 8

Mason

I told Miles I couldn't spend the day with him because I had to write, and even though it really was my plan for the day, it was a lie.

That kiss on the porch scared the bejesus out of me.

He says all the right things.

He looks at me in a way that makes me weak in the knees.

His kiss…well, I'm still feeling it this morning.

His rough hands couldn't have been gentler, holding me as if I were precious.

I've had plenty of kisses in my life, but none have ever felt like they were taking my breath away while filling me with everything I'll ever need to survive this crazy roller coaster of life.

It was a moment unlike any other before it.

It was perfect yet too much all at once.

I can still feel every touch.

Earlier in the evening, hearing him talk about the redhead in

Pendleton brought up a flash flood of Grant's cheating ways, but they had vanished by the time we hit the dance floor.

So why did they have to come rushing back on the porch? Why did I pull back from the most romantic encounter I've ever experienced?

Because it felt too good? Too right?

Because it scared the hell out of me.

I could feel my heart breaking already.

I know how I felt when things ended with Grant, so the moment my lips touched his, I knew immediately how things would feel at the end if I fell for Miles. I already know my ending with him would hurt so much worse than the pain my ex had inflicted on me.

Even though staying in to write today was a lame excuse not to accept his offer, I really did intend to work. But that was before he kissed me. Okay, technically, *I* kissed him, but I've been rattled ever since.

After staring at my computer for far too long, it's time to wave my white flag and accept the fact that I am getting nowhere, and I need to get out of the house.

I may live on the "other side" of town, but the heart of Eastlyn is only a mile or so away, so I grab my camera and my bag and head out into the hot August sun to find some inspiration.

The first business on my end of town is a quaint little antique shop and as I snap my first picture of the awning I decide I'm not just taking pictures outside today, I'm going to go into every place I haven't been to yet.

I spend the next hour and a half stopping into every business on Main Street. The entire time, I picture Miles growing up in this idyllic town with his idyllic family and lifelong group of friends who are just as close to him as his family.

I can see him running around causing havoc all over town.

With every picture I take, I see Miles.

The steps of the Eastlyn Community Church at the end of Main Street.

The striped pole outside Mel's Barber Shop.

The wooden benches in front of The General Store.

The Eastlyn Brewing Company is represented everywhere you look. The iconic green and white logo, featuring a dock with two empty Adirondack chairs facing a lake is featured in the windows of The Verdict, The Jury Room, The General Store, Ken's Pizzeria, and just about every other business in town in some way, shape, or form.

The town is proud, as they should be.

The focal point of town is the courthouse. For such a small town, the courthouse is much bigger than I would have expected. But it does house all the government offices with the police station right next door. Fittingly, there is a donut shop next to the police station called Holding Cell Donuts.

I'm sure Miles has eaten his share of donuts from the Holding Cell, but I can't help but wonder if the town playboy has also spent time in an *actual* holding cell at the police station. I know he's eaten plenty at the diner across the street and had his fair share of beer at the bar on the other corner of the street, so I wouldn't be surprised if he rounded out his time spent with all four corners of Main and 3rd by spending a night or two with the Eastlyn P.D.

I find it hard to believe his charm works on *everyone* he meets.

With every picture I take, my decision to come to Eastlyn is reaffirmed. This quaint little town feels like it was pulled right out of my imagination. It's exactly what I was thinking of when the idea for my latest romance series came to my mind. Only the man at the center of my story wasn't a blond farm boy who looks good in backward baseball caps and kisses like a lothario.

I think I'll be scrapping my small-town judge idea and change directions when it comes to the hero of my story.

Feeling inspired, I pop into The Jury Room, and funnily

enough, I get seated at the same booth where Miles and I had lunch. Pulling my journal out of my bag, I begin spilling words onto the page like a woman possessed. Snacking on my fries while burning through the pages of my outline, I'm excited to get back home to my laptop.

Too excited to wait for the check.

Dropping a twenty to cover my five-dollar snack, I have a new spring in my step when I leave the diner. I'm anxious to get home and get to work. When the words come, there isn't anything I can do, I have to write!

The moment I walk through the door, I change into my customary all-night writing uniform of leggings and an oversized sweater. Thank goodness Katie has air conditioning because Eastern Oregon is an oven in the summer, and there's no way my writing attire would work if not.

I plot. I drink wine. I outline. I drink more wine.

I write all night long, finally calling it quits around four o'clock in the morning, so when I hear a lawn mower at ten o'clock, I'm far from pleased. Especially when it sounds like it's coming from right out in front of the house. Please tell me Katie doesn't have a landscaper she forgot to tell me about.

Pausing long enough to make sure I'm fully dressed, I march to the front of the house and nearly blind myself when I rip back the curtain and the blazing summer sun attempts to burn my corneas and leave me blind.

Even with my hand above my eyes to block some of the daylight assaulting my vision, it's of no use. I can't see who the hell is on my lawn.

I close my eyes for a few seconds, hoping to bring them to life, and when I open them again, I let out a scream that would wake the dead. Miles Montgomery is so close to the window; the glass is the only thing keeping us apart.

Standing on the other side of the glass waving and smiling like an idiot is my resident handyman.

"Did I wake you up, Sleeping Beauty?"

He's yelling through the window, but I can hear him just fine since he's pressing his face to the glass like a child.

"Didn't you mow two days ago?"

"Not mowing, edging. Didn't have everything I needed the other day, so I thought I'd come back and finish up. You won't even know I'm here."

"If only."

"Sorry, what was that? I couldn't hear you," he continues to yell.

"You really don't need to do all this," I yell back at him through the window like a fool. "You were only supposed to fix a board on the back porch. Do you ever work?"

"Damn, Mason, I didn't think it was possible, but you actually look more beautiful right now than you did when I left you the other night."

As soon as the words are out of his mouth, the mess on top of my head and the smeared makeup under my eyes reflect back at me in the window.

I've never looked worse.

I. Could. Die.

"Nice try, Miles. It was a long night. I know I look terrible, so you don't have to be mean."

"Mason, you have no idea what you..." He trails off, not finishing his sentence.

Frustrated, he flips his baseball cap around and wipes his hand over his face.

"Listen, I'm just gonna get back to it. Sorry I woke you up... but it was totally worth it."

And there it is.

That smile and those stupid dimples.

I was so busy trying to ignore him the first night I met him that I somehow missed the dimples, but standing here in the bright as hell morning light, I can't take my eyes off them. Well, until he moves, distracting me, and when I glance up at his eyes, even through the window, I can see the gold flecks dancing with satisfaction in his copper-colored eyes because he knows his words and that beautiful face of his have caught me off guard.

"See ya later, Mase."

He walks away and hits me with another blow when I get a look at his ass in those jeans. I've always appreciated a nice denim-covered ass, but I have never seen a pair of jeans filled out quite like his. His jeans, his dimples, his eyes, and most certainly, his backward baseball cap have all been featured in my journal on numerous occasions.

I always have two journals on me. One for my current work in progress and one that I spew all my thoughts about life into. I guess it would be considered a diary, but I call it a journal.

Because I'm a grown-up.

Like a girl whose first crush finally acknowledged her existence, I practically skip to the bathroom to turn on the shower. I'm acting all aflutter because the hot guy in town thinks I'm pretty.

Maybe I'm not so grown up after all.

Let's be real, it feels like more than a playground crush.

I can honestly say that for the first time in my life, I am hot and bothered and bouncing out of my skin wondering what in the world he was going to say when he stopped himself. It's killing me not to know.

As I begin to step into the shower, I see myself in the mirror and laugh at how bad I look. Actually, I look like I was up all night having sex.

Complimenting me in my current state takes charm to a level even I've never experienced.

Come to think of it, maybe he needs glasses?

Either way, here's hoping the shower calms me down enough to act my age, and more importantly, I stay in long enough for him to be gone when I get out.

My intention was to take my time, but the butterflies (I see them as pink and purple and maybe even with some glitter thrown in there) are causing havoc in my stomach, keeping me on edge and rushing to finish. My brain may tell me I want him to be gone, but the dopamine-laced butterflies racing around my insides know this is a lie. I can't get ready fast enough in hopes that I get to see him again.

The first thing I notice once I've toweled off and slipped into my robe is that it's quiet. The new friends in my stomach start to slowly float away since the silence most likely means he's gone. Bummed as I may be, I still keep replaying our interaction in the front window over and over, finding it hard not to smile at myself while doing my makeup.

I'm just about to turn on the blow dryer when I freeze. Hearing what sounds like the barking of a dog coming from the backyard.

Holy crap.

That sounded like Lou.

Was that Lou?

Is he still here?

No way!

I run out of the bathroom like a woman with my hair on fire so I can look out the kitchen window, and sure enough, there they are. Two of the most handsome bachelors of Eastlyn, Oregon.

Lou is up on his back legs going crazy over something up one of the giant pine trees in the backyard, doing what dogs do, but his daddy has just dropped a big bag of soil on the ground and is using the bottom of his T-shirt to wipe the sweat from his face, revealing his stomach.

Oh. My. Goodness.

The six-pack.

The V.

The way his jeans...

Oh, snap. I've been busted.

The arrogant smile gracing his lips says he knows I was looking, and not only was I looking but I clearly like what I see.

Shit!

Still behaving like a preteen, I run out of the room with my face on fire this time and slam the bathroom door behind me, hiding from the hot jock who caught me staring.

I am such an idiot.

This time, I actually do take my time blowing out my hair and getting dressed. Heading back to the kitchen to feed my grumbling stomach, I force myself not to look out back. But when I see the bottom shelf of the fridge lined with bottles of water, I can't help but think how thirsty Miles must be out there in the summer heat.

Glancing out the window, it looks like he's cleaning up, and I begin to panic, thinking he might be leaving when all I've done so far today is stare at him through a variety of windows.

I'm pathetic.

I grab two bottles of water and a bowl and take a deep breath before opening the door to the backyard.

"You guys thirsty?" I yell, holding the cold beverages up.

Lou bounds across the yard at full speed, his tail wagging and tongue dangling probably thinking I have a treat of some sort.

A few feet before the shepherd gets to me, Miles yells, "Lou, down!" and just like that, he stops in his tracks and lies down. He's panting, tongue hanging out, but he's doing exactly what his daddy told him to do.

I throw one of the ice-cold bottles at his dad, whose long strides have him heading across the grass toward me, and then I put the bowl in front of my new furry friend and fill it for him.

"Here you go, buddy. You've been working hard out here, haven't you?" I say, scratching him behind the ears while he laps up his water.

"Oh, yeah. He's been workin' real hard at chasin critters,

sniffing the fence line, and peeing everywhere. I swear he never runs out."

Standing to acknowledge Miles, I make the mistake of turning around just as he lifts his T-shirt again. This time, I'm wise enough to look away the second I get my first glimpse of that V.

I certainly don't want to be caught drooling again. Man, that was embarrassing. I'm waiting for him to bring it up because I know he will. It's what he does. He's just waiting for the right moment to mortify me.

"Thanks for the water."

"Thanks for all the manual labor. Does Katie know what you've been up to?"

"I mentioned some stuff I thought needed to be done after I fixed the board on the porch, and she said she was cool with me working on things."

"Well, aren't you a Boy Scout?"

"Truth?" He whispers as though he has a secret the dog can't hear.

"Uh, okay?"

"Lou wanted a reason to come see you. He thought if we hung around long enough, you'd finally come out and talk to us. Looks like it worked. Smart dog, eh?"

Oh, what this man does to me. I really wish he'd turn his baseball cap around because when he says things like that, and I have full view of his eyes, I don't stand a chance.

"Lou came up with that all on his own?"

"He's advanced. What can I say?"

Lou's up and dripping water all over my feet, so I give him a scratch. "Are you advanced, sweetheart?" I swear the dog smiles back at me. "Of course you are."

"So, what have you been up to since I saw you last?" he asks.

Surprising myself, I kinda want to show him my pictures from yesterday.

"Wanna see?"

"Of course!"

His enthusiasm is infectious and has me skipping inside, but then I remember I haven't invited him in, and when I reach the back door, I see him still standing in the yard with Lou.

"Well, you coming in or what?"

"Honey, you don't have to ask me twice."

I beat him in and pop open my laptop at the kitchen table, and before I'm logged in, they've joined me inside.

"So, yesterday I spent the first part of my day wandering around town and taking pictures. Pictures inspire me. I usually make a vision board and put it up in my office back home, so I have my inspiration in front of me while I work."

"Very cool, let's see what you got here."

He scoots his chair closer, and I can smell the outdoors, a little bit of sweat, and something else that makes the combination of it all a bit heady.

As we scroll through the pictures, he gives me a brief history of each location and shares some personal stories from his childhood. Not surprisingly, he's a great storyteller and has me in stitches in one moment and teary-eyed the next.

"I see you have lots of pictures of the Eastlyn Beer Company sign. Any special reason?"

"Well, you already know it's my favorite beer and can be hard to come by at most places on the East Coast. So, it's sort of like when you go to New York, you take a picture of the Statue of Liberty or the Empire State Building. In Philadelphia, you take a picture of the Liberty Bell so…"

"You're saying Eastlyn Beer is your Liberty Bell?"

"No…well, yes. I don't know. I'm just saying it's a landmark that means something to me. And for some reason, I love the logo. Something about those two empty chairs grabs at me. I've always imagined sitting there with a special someone while we drink our beers. I don't know, there's just something about it. I know, I know, it's a beer logo, and it's a silly thing to be drawn to."

He pushes a loose hair behind my ear, and quietly says, "It's not silly at all. I think it's kind of beautiful."

The close proximity and the quiet in his voice are enough to send me into a screaming orgasm all on their own, but with the light touch of his fingers against the side of my face, I'm having to press my thighs together to try to calm the ache he's causing with no effort at all.

"Mason, let me show you *my* Eastlyn. If you're looking for inspiration, we need to get you off Main Street and show you how much more there is to the town. I have to be in Portland this weekend, and I have meetings I can't miss most days next week, but I'll have time between if that works? And next weekend, I'm free."

"Can I see the farm?"

"You know what, I can do better. How about watching the sun rise over the farm? Tomorrow morning? I can't spend the whole day, but I'm good until after lunch."

"Are you sure? If you're too busy with your meetings, it can wait."

"Tomorrow, things don't get started until the afternoon. How about we hang at the farm for a bit, and then we'll start our tour Monday after I get back?"

"That works for me."

"I'll pick you up at ten till five?"

"In the morning?"

"You good with black coffee?"

I nod my reply, wondering if I should rethink our morning excursion. I mean, who gets up that early?

"Good. It's a date. See you bright and early."

And just like that, he takes his dog and walks out of the house as though he didn't just say we were going on a date.

Let the roller coaster ride begin.

CHAPTER 9

Mason

Miles sent me a text last night to let me know it could be a little chilly this morning, and I should dress accordingly. So, here I am at 4:45 a.m. in a T-shirt and flannel, jeans, and Dr. Martens with my camera slung across my chest, pacing in front of the living room window waiting for *my date* to show up. Getting my anxiety out by wearing a trench into Katie's floors seems the only way to keep my nerves at bay.

When the headlights from his truck illuminate the driveway I don't wait for him to come to the door. I need to get out of the house and get this sunrise started before I combust. I'm halfway to his truck before he's out of the cab.

"Wow, I wouldn't have thought of you as a morning person," he whispers, so we don't disturb the neighbors, as he runs across the driveway to meet me halfway.

"Hardly. I can't remember the last time I was up this early," I whisper back.

"Well, here." He holds out a silver thermos and leans in close, filling my head with the scent of soap and Miles. "This should help, but be careful. It's hot."

He can't be real.

I keep waiting for him to do something douchey but no such luck.

"Thank you. Did you make it?" I ask, screwing off the top to take in the fresh brewed coffee smell on my way to the passenger side of his big Dodge.

"Sure did, but you might want to put the lid back on before you get in. Lou's bound to be excited to see you, and I'd hate for you to spill hot coffee all over yourself."

He opens my door while I put the top to my thermos back on.

When I climb in, Lou proves his dad right and tries to hop up in my lap, causing Miles to lean over me to push him back. He says something to the dog, but I don't hear it because he's so close. His left hand is braced on the seat behind me while he leans in front of me to use his right hand to push the dog back.

He smells like he just got out of the shower, and with his head sans baseball cap this morning, nothing prohibits my view of him. His short hair doesn't need a lot of work to get where it is, but it's clear he styled his waves today.

Before he moves away, he looks at me.

Really looks at me.

He doesn't say a word.

He doesn't flash one of his knowing smiles.

He just looks at me, and my world starts spinning so fast I feel dizzy sitting in my seat. I almost grab onto him to right myself, but he pulls away before I get the chance.

Whoa.

The intensity of that look sticks with me all the way to the farm. Neither of us speaks and by the time Miles parks the truck, the sky is ever so slowly lightening.

"Ready?"

"Can't wait," I say, lifting my camera up in reply.

"Let's go."

He gets out and opens the back door to the king cab to let his furry child out of the truck. Lou runs ahead toward the rows of hops.

Joining him in front of the truck, I question what we're doing. "We aren't watching from the truck?"

"No way. We can do better than that. Come on," he says, grabbing my hand.

I don't pull away.

Besides, I can't see a thing out here. Safety first and all that.

"Where are we headed?"

"Just a little farther."

"Miles, this is crazy. We could have just sat in the bed of the truck."

"Mason, I don't think you're ready to be in any kind of bed with me, so let's not go there."

I attempt to pull my hand away from his, but he doesn't let me, thank goodness.

"It was a joke, Mason. Besides, we're here, and this will be so much better."

The flashlight on his phone illuminates our surroundings, revealing a huge John Deere tractor. It's just as I've always imagined. That unique green color, big tires, and from what I can see through the plexiglass windows, one seat.

"Miles, we aren't both going to fit in there."

"Sure we will."

He steps up and onto the tractor opening the glass door and climbing inside.

"Come on in, City Mouse," he says, shining his phone at the rungs in front of the giant tire.

There must be more room in there than I think, so I climb up the side of the tractor only to find I've been hoodwinked.

He pats his lap. "See, plenty of room."

"Miles Montgomery, you are impossible."

"Listen, there isn't a better place to watch the sunrise. You'll thank me later."

"Miles…"

"Mason, sit down, or you're gonna miss it."

He opens his arms, inviting me to sit, so of course, I take a seat on his lap. Without hesitation, he wraps his arms around me, and it feels well…perfect. Like we'd done it a million times before.

"You know I've sat in this field, in this very tractor and watched the sun rise more times than I can count, but I can already guarantee this one is gonna be the best one yet."

There isn't anything I can say to his beautiful statement.

The sky is like a dark canvas laid out before us slowly being painted by Mother Nature. The orange glow from the morning sun leisurely makes its presence known while turning the skies above it a shade of blue that changes with every second that passes.

Sinking into him, I allow myself to wrap my hands around his currently encircling me.

I don't know what his other sunrises here at Montgomery Farms have been like, but for my first, I'd have to say it's pretty magical.

We sit in silence watching the beauty before us until the last bit of the sun fills the hazy summer sky rising high above the Oregon skyline.

"Told you," he whispers in my ear.

I know what he's referring to, but I ask him anyway. "Told me what?"

"This one would be the best one yet."

He gives me a little squeeze, and we admire the view a while longer, not wanting it to be over. The blur of Lou running past makes us both chuckle.

"I wish I had even half of his energy," he says, and much to my dismay, he releases me. "Come on, let's go for a walk so you can take some pictures."

"Crap! I completely forgot to take pictures!"

"Well, it's still pretty. Hop on out and take them without that dirty windshield in front of you. But first say cheese," he says, lifting his phone to take a selfie of the two of us.

I'd never ask, but I sure hope he sends me a copy.

He's right, the shots I'm getting are perfect. Once I've gotten what I need, I turn around to find him leaning against the tractor watching me, so I lift the camera and take a picture to capture him in the moment.

He doesn't smile.

He doesn't say anything.

He just watches me watching him.

Thankfully, Lou barks, jumping in his daddy's face to get his attention. He reaches in his back pocket and pulls out a tan canvas toy of some sort and throws it off into the distance for Lou to chase after.

"You're a good daddy."

He shrugs. "Come on, let's go get our coffee out of the truck, and we can go for a walk. I'll show you around."

"I'd love that. But what about Lou?"

"He'll be back in a flash. Don't you worry about him. He knows this place better than anyone."

Once we have our coffee, he starts with the basics, explaining that we're on a hops farm, and that it's currently harvest season and the area we're in has already been harvested. This would be why this section of the farm seems a bit sparse. He tells me the unusually warm weather this year brought harvest season on several weeks early. It's caused things around the farm to spring into their busy time of year sooner than they usually do.

"How can you tell when it's time?"

"Come here, I'll show you." He takes me by the hand and walks me over to one of the rows not yet harvested.

"Here, give this a squeeze."

His fingers are on what looks like a small green pine cone. I place my fingers where his had been, giving it a gentle squeeze.

"This is the actual hop flower, but it's also called a cone. See how that feels springy yet dry and papery?"

"Uh, huh."

"That's the first sign. Now pick that cone off and roll it between your hands. That sticky yellow substance you feel on the stem is called lupulin, and that's sign number two."

"And is there a third sign?"

I can't believe I'm sincerely wanting to know, but I am intrigued.

"There is. It's the smell. They usually smell almost like grass before they ripen. Once they lose that grassy smell, it's time."

I take an inhale of the hop in my hand, and it almost burns my throat. "Whoa, that's pungent."

"Almost spicy, right?"

"I guess that's the right word. It's just stronger than I expected."

We start walking again while I roll the cone between my fingers and listen to him go on about the harvest process and his concerns for how the warmer climate may change the way they farm. And I'm hanging on his every word.

The other side of the farm that he'll take me to later is home to hazelnuts. It's almost harvest season for the hazelnuts as well, but that season will go for a month longer than the hops once it begins.

If you had told me I would find crop information interesting a couple of weeks ago, I wouldn't have believed it, but I I'm a sponge soaking it all in. He's knowledgeable and passionate and actually very smart.

"This means a lot to you, doesn't it?"

"This land…this farm…have been in our family for decades. It's home. It's what I know."

"Don't most farmers work from sunrise till sundown? You seem to have a lot of free time on your hands."

"You aren't wrong about that. Farmers are some of the hardest working people you'll ever meet. We've been fortunate. In the past ten years, we've found ourselves in a place where my family is spending most of our time running the farm in the business sense. We are lucky enough to have a great crew working for us who do all the hard work."

"When you say family, do you have siblings who help out?"

"Stacci, my sister, went to college and never came back. It's just my parents and me, but to be honest, my parents are pretty much retired, so I guess it's really me that runs things."

"How do you feel about that? Is it something you would have chosen for yourself or do you feel like you don't have a choice?"

"Nah, I've always got a choice. In fact, this afternoon, my parents and I are meeting to talk about making some pretty big changes. My parents and I agree on most everything, but at the moment, we aren't seeing eye to eye on the next steps."

He opens his arms to the endless rows of what I now know are called bines of green hop plants. Lifting my camera, I take a picture of him with his passion behind him. The green landscape of the farm surrounding him coming nowhere near the natural beauty of the man. Especially, when he talks about this land.

"Did you just take my picture?"

It's my turn to shrug a reply.

"Am I gonna see that as your screensaver on your phone later? I am, aren't I?"

"You are an idiot."

"It's okay. I won't tell anybody that you're infatuated with me. The feeling's mutual."

And there it is. Miles Montgomery stopping me in my tracks with his charming words yet again.

Embarrassed, I turn away from him, lifting my camera to take a picture, but he knows as well as I do it's to shield his view of my flushed face.

Lou drops his toy at my feet, and I throw it for my new bestie. Because that's what friends are for, right?

"So, you and your parents are pretty close then? This business stuff doesn't get in the way?"

"I love my parents. We may not agree on what to do with the farm, but we're still tight as can be. I rarely miss a Sunday dinner."

"I can't imagine spending time with my family because I want to and not because it's expected of me. You have no idea how lucky you are."

He turns back in the direction of the truck, and I follow his lead, only now realizing the truck is so far away it's no longer in view. Sweet Lou comes up from the rear and slows down to walk beside us with his toy in his mouth.

"I'm sorry things aren't better with your family, Mase. Has it always been that way?"

"Well, I'm an only child, but I'm not a boy, so there's that."

"Thank God for that." He gives me a wink, sending shivers down my back in the very best kind of way.

"I still got the boy name, though. Lucky me."

"Nah, I like it. It's kinda hot."

"Anyway, my parents come from money and are pretty old school," I say, ignoring him.

"More details please."

I hate talking about my parents. In fact, I never do, so why I feel so comfortable talking to him about them? I have no idea.

"Okay, let me find the right words. Um…my parents are of the mindset that even though women go to college and get degrees, their real purpose is to look pretty on their husband's arm while not using the degree they worked so hard for. You know, our skills are apparently better used to make a beautiful home and of course one to two perfect children. I was pretty much a used-up spinster at the ripe old age of twenty-six."

"Understood. So, how do they feel about your career?"

Our pace is slow, taking our time walking up and down the rows of hops. He picks a leaf here and there while he listens.

"That's a bit of a loaded question."

"How so?"

"Well, how my parents feel about my career, let me rephrase that. How my father feels about my career changes, depending on the circumstances. My mom…she feels whatever her husband tells her she feels."

"Ouch."

"You have no idea."

"I'd like to, though, so why don't you enlighten me?"

Miles Montgomery sure can be sweet.

"Well, before I was a success, they were embarrassed by what I chose to write. Let's just say, Sunday dinners with my parents, if we had had them, would have consisted of them telling me what a disappointment I was to them, and how I was shaming them by writing X-rated trash."

"X-rated, you say? Maybe I should check out your work."

"That's the thing. They act like I write porn, but I don't. I write about real life, and real life includes people falling in love, and like most people in love, sex is usually a part of the equation."

"I like the way you think, lady. Your parents, however, sound a little stuffy, if you don't mind me saying."

"Not at all. Your assessment would be extremely accurate. The thing is, when the series sold and got lots of notice, they were suddenly proud and claimed to have always known I had it in me or some crap like that. Then, when things ended with my ex, I was wasting my life and letting the family down. Merging my family with his would have been a great investment for both of our families' legacies. My career…my happiness…didn't matter. So, not only did I lose the guy but I also lost my family. Why?

Because I was just a pawn in their nasty scheme, and in the end, I was the least important person involved."

"So your parents just wrote you off like that?"

"Not sure, because I wrote them off first."

"Was it hard?"

"I wish I could say it was, but it really wasn't. I spent my entire life being told to sit up straight, smile, only speak when spoken to, and without exception, to never have my own opinion. When you find out you've done everything they've told you to do your entire life only for them to be on the side of the person who betrays you and breaks your heart, it makes it easier to walk away."

We've reached the truck, and he walks to the passenger side door but pauses before opening it for me, shoving his hands in his front pockets.

"Mason?"

"Miles?"

"I'm really sorry your life has been full of assholes who didn't see you for all that you are."

My heart isn't sure what to do with all of his kindness. I think I feel more sure of myself when he's being a smart-ass.

"Thank you. I appreciate it, but you don't have to feel sorry for me."

"I only speak the truth, Mason. Now, how do you feel about hazelnuts?"

And just like that, he lightens the mood and lights up my heart.

He drives us a few minutes away to the hazelnut crops, and we spend the next hour walking and talking about everything and nothing. I swear the green on the leaves is deeper and more beautiful when you're walking through them with him as your guide. His love for everything surrounding us knows no bounds, and I'm seeing colors I don't remember ever seeing before.

By the time we're back in the truck, I know all about The

Crew, the locals around town, and his childhood growing up running through the fields here at Montgomery Farms.

Yes, he is without a doubt charming, but he's also incredibly down to earth.

After a trip through the hazelnuts, he takes me to what they call The House. This is the house he grew up in, only now it serves as home base to the farm. He shows me his office and introduces me to his team. There are sleeping quarters the team can use while the hours are long during harvest season, and they even have a fully stocked kitchen.

It's more than clear the Montgomerys care about their employees.

Activity has picked up in the hours since we arrived. You can see hop harvesters and top cutters out in the distance. Crazy that I know what hop harvesters and top cutters are, but I do, thanks to the infectious enthusiasm my tour guide has for the topic.

What is also infectious is how everyone feels about Miles as we walk through The House.

They may call him "boss," but there is a genuine family feel between all of the men working at Montgomery Farms. Miles asks about their families and knows all of their children's names. It is a small town, and I'm sure everyone knows everyone, but this feels more like a family than a business. The crap they fling at each other is pretty fun to witness, too, especially with their boss as the ringleader.

Something else I'm shocked I didn't notice until well into our visit is that a lot of the guys are wearing Eastlyn Brewing Company hats or T-shirts. There is EBC signage all over The House as well. In fact, there is just as much paraphernalia for EBC as there is for Montgomery Farms.

Quite some time later after doing some quick paperwork, then going over some equipment issues with Peter and some of the other guys, Miles says he needs to grab something out of the kitchen, and as I follow him down the hall, I ask the obvious.

"Miles, I cannot believe I'm just now catching on to this, but does Montgomery Farms grow the hops used in EBC?"

Looking over his shoulder with the corners of his mouth lifted ever so slightly, he gives me a wink. "I was wondering when you might notice that."

"Shut up! Are you telling me I was walking through rows and rows of hops that are going to end up in my favorite adult beverage?"

He chuckles at my excitement. "Indeed."

"Miles, I touched them."

His laughter reverberates off the seventies era burnt sienna walls adorned with a rooster wallpaper border. Not to mention the cracked Formica countertops that lend to the old-school feel.

It's perfect.

"You really like beer, don't you?" he says, opening the refrigerator. One of the only upgrades in the room.

There's no stopping the smile stretching across my face. "I do. But I'm not an alcoholic or anything. I usually have one or two and call it good. My parents and Grant frowned upon a woman of my stature drinking beer. So of course I would drink it every chance I got. And then one day, I was in LA visiting a friend, and I asked the bartender to bring me his favorite beer on tap, and he brought me an EBC, and my life was changed forever."

He closes the refrigerator door and gets close. So close, there are only a couple of very small, very electric inches between us.

"What you're really saying is, in a roundabout way, I changed your life forever," he whispers.

Oh, shit. That *is* kind of what I just said.

He's good.

I should be embarrassed, but I'm not. I'm giddy and a little turned on at our proximity.

"I guess you did," I whisper back. Leaning into him, I eliminate the space between us. "Thank you."

To show my appreciation, I gently press my lips to his, and he kisses me back ever so lightly yet pulls away before things get heated.

"You're welcome, City Mouse."

His breath flutters across my face. He's teasing me because he knows I want more of his lips.

Miles Montgomery has me all tangled up.

Tangled up with feelings I shouldn't be feeling. But there isn't a thing I can do to stop it. And I cannot deny the fact that the man stealing my heart without even trying is also the man whose blood, sweat, and tears go into one of my favorite things isn't a pretty crazy coincidence.

"Come on, let's go have lunch." He takes my hand, lacing his fingers with mine, and guides me back through the house and out to the truck.

He doesn't say much as we drive to a quiet part of the farm. Once he's parked, we hop out, and he drops the tailgate and spreads out a thick blanket.

"Hop on up," he says, patting the blanket. "Need a boost?"

I jump up and take my place in answer to his question of me needing a boost.

He puts a soft shell cooler next to me and then hoists himself up on the other side of it.

"Lunch is served, milady."

My heart is swelling with every kind gesture he makes. He's thought of everything, yet he hasn't made any chaste moves. He's been nothing but a gentleman whereas I was the one to kiss him on the porch the other night and then again in the house a few minutes ago. Either I'm reading things wrong and he doesn't feel the same way I do, or he's really trying to do this right.

"Hungry?"

"Did you make this yourself?"

"Yes, ma'am. Today's menu includes cheese, crackers, sandwiches, sliced apples, and your choice of soda or bottled water."

"Sounds perfect."

Just like everything else about you.

He lays out a board he pulled out of the cooler and spreads out our tailgate picnic. When I compare the tranquil beauty of being out here on the farm and the quiet contentment that comes with it to the noise and nonstop rush of living in the city I'm surprised to find I don't think I could pick one over the other when it comes to which way of life is more idyllic.

Both are filled with hopes and dreams; they're just achieved differently. Miles's dreams may not be achieved wearing a suit and making deals day in and day out, but he's just as fulfilled making his come true by working the land. Actually, he doesn't seem to work the land much these days, but still.

"Dive in."

Miles starts with his sandwich, and I follow suit since he hasn't led me astray so far. My legs naturally swing back and forth off the edge of the tailgate as I take the first bite of my classic turkey and cheese sandwich topped with lettuce, tomato, and honey Dijon mustard that gives it a little bit of a kick.

"So good," I mumble as the old-school white bread sticks to the roof of my mouth.

"Glad you like it."

"Miles, today has been great," I say after swallowing my bite down. "Thank you so much for sharing your world with me."

"My pleasure."

"I mean it. From the sunrise to this kick-ass lunch, it's one of the best days I've had since…well, I can't even remember a day when I've felt so content. So happy. Thank you."

His head tilts to the side just like Lou's does when you ask him if he wants a treat.

"Mason, I have to say as happy as it makes me that I could make you feel what you're feeling today, it hurts my heart to hear you say you can't remember the last time you felt like this. Darlin', you deserve a lot more out of life than that."

He's right.

He's always right.

What do I even say to that?

"This is great cheese; what kind is it?"

Seriously, you're asking him about his cheese right now?

"It's cheese, Mason. Tell me, who do you spend most of your time with back in New York?"

"Friends."

"Tell me about them."

"Tell you about my friends? You mean, besides my journal?"

"Why not? You've met plenty of mine. We'll get to the journal later."

Is he for real?

"Let's see…um…well, as you know, most of the friends I grew up with or that I thought were closest to me screwed me over. I still have a couple of trustworthy girlfriends from my old life, and I see them from time to time."

"I'm glad to hear that."

"Thanks," I reply shyly before continuing. "I have a really great group of friends I met through work. A lot of them work in publishing, and even though I'm an author and they are actual publishers and editors or work in some other capacity in the publishing world, we all hit it off. We have a standing date every Thursday night. Whoever is in town and available shows up, and we have drinks and dinner, and we talk for hours at a time. It's a pretty great group of ladies. I feel like I've found my tribe with them."

"Do I even want to know what you all talk about for hours on end every single week?"

"Probably not. But let's see, we talk about books, men, royal weddings, work, how much we love them, but don't need men to be happy…"

Miles interrupts me after my last comment. "Wait a second, go back a tick. So, are you one of the ones who loves men but doesn't need one to be happy?"

Well, at least I know he's listening.

"Yes and no. I mean, I would love to build a life with a man who is my best friend and who sets me on fire between the sheets. A man I can share beers with on the EBC dock when I'm old. Who doesn't want that?"

Tearing my gaze from the splendor in front of me, I chance a look at an even more breathtaking landscape when our eyes meet.

He lifts an eyebrow in intrigue. "Go on."

"But, let's face it. I don't need a man to take care of me or to make me happy. I've made my own money. I have a kick-ass career and an apartment in one of the greatest cities in the world. I've created my own brand and have succeeded in an industry that is oversaturated, yet I've found a way to stand out and make my own path. I'm strong on my own, Miles. A lot of men find my *confidence* to be a little off-putting, you know?"

"Actually, I don't. I think your confidence looks pretty damn good on you."

Be still my thunderous heart and the butterflies fluttering to life inside my chest.

"Any man can say that, but when it comes to being in a relationship with a strong woman, it may not be quite so appealing."

"This is just another example of where I'm different from the other men in your life. Your confidence and independence are sexy as hell, if you ask me."

He throws a cracker in his mouth as though there is nothing else to be said.

Visions of clearing the tailgate of our lunch and mounting him in the bed of the truck speed through my brain. I know it's a bad decision, so I don't act upon it, but damn, I want him in the worst way.

The conversation has gone silent, and even out here in the vastness of the farm, you would have to sledgehammer through the layers of lust hovering between us.

He contains himself much better than I do, but I see it in his eyes. He's determined to prove himself to me. I find this makes him even more attractive.

Dammit!

Checking his watch, he slides off the tailgate and begins to gather the remnants of our lunch. "As much as I hate to cut this short, I have a meeting with my parents soon, so I best be getting you home, City Mouse."

I shouldn't, but I love the stupid nickname he's given me.

A sucker. That's what I am. I'm letting him charm me. Knowingly. And I don't care. There's a sincerity to him that I want so desperately to be true.

"No problem. I've taken up enough of your day."

"Nonsense, this will have been the best part of my day, and if I had my way, you would take up the rest of it too, but duty calls."

Without warning, his hands land on my waist, and he lifts me off the tailgate to place me on my feet. It takes everything I have not to wrap my legs around his waist and never let go.

As much as it pains me to admit, even if only to myself, he's going about our time together in all the right ways. If it weren't for the lingering stares, sweet words, and obvious gestures, I'd think he just wants us to be friends, but unless I'm completely delusional, I find that hard to believe.

Once we're packed up, and Lou is in the back seat, we drive back through the property, and I can't stop the endless questions in my head from falling out of my mouth. In fact, my questions and our conversation don't end until we pull up in front of Katie's house.

I'm busy saying goodbye to his sweet pup in the back seat when Miles opens my door for me, but he doesn't step aside so I can get out. He stands right there, inches away looking me right in the eye, like he always does. Never shying away from me.

"I hope you got some good pictures today?"

Struggling for breath anytime we're this close is becoming a common occurrence.

Answering a simple question is taking a much higher level of concentration than it should.

Not letting myself get consumed by whatever it is that makes Miles, well, Miles is quite the task, but I manage to pull myself together.

"I'm sure I did. I can't wait to get on my computer and check them out."

Taking my hand and stepping to the side, he says, "Well, don't let me slow you down. I'll walk you to the door."

Crap! He thinks I'm trying to get rid of him.

Nice job, Mason.

I've unlocked the front door and can't think of anything to prolong our time together, so reluctantly, I turn to say goodbye.

"City Mouse, I hope you've got a bunch of empty pages in that journal of yours because I'm going to show you the Eastlyn I was raised on. I hope you're ready?" His soft lips lightly brush my cheek before he rushes back to his truck and drives away with a wave.

Am I ready to see his Eastlyn?

Just as I've done since the fourth grade, I open my journal as soon as I've made my way inside and spend the next hour detailing my day and all the feelings that came along with it.

I probably shouldn't have mentioned my journal when Miles asked me to tell him about all my closest friends because let's face it, I tell her everything.

CHAPTER 10

Mason

Dear Journal,

TODAY, Miles began what he's calling his "Raised On It" tour of Eastlyn.

We started a lot later today, and he only had about three hours to spend with me, but it was great. Not sure anything could match our sunrise from yesterday, but every minute spent with him somehow seems better than the last.

It hasn't gone unnoticed by me that he's extremely busy with harvest and whatever business deals it is he and his parents have been meeting about. I haven't said it to him, but it means a lot to me that he would take what little time he has to show me around town.

Since I'd already been to the farm, he took me to the schools he grew up in today. It's still summer break for the kids, so they were empty.

However, Miles had the keys to the K-8 school as well as the high school and could open any room he wanted to show me.

Maybe he's the mayor of Eastlyn, and somehow it hasn't come up in conversation? I can't think of any other reason to explain why he just happened to have the keys to all of the schools in town.

When I asked this exact question, he just said he had friends in high places.

I have a sneaking suspicion there's more to this local farm boy than he or anyone else is telling me.

He showed me each and every classroom he had over the years, gave me teachers' names, and shared stories of pulling pigtails on the playground and stealing kisses in the library. We even went for a walk on the football field where he played for the Eastlyn Eagles.

The gleam in his eye while he shared his stories was incredibly endearing. Sweet. And yes, charming. It's also more than evident he loved growing up here, and I think it's safe to say he loved his school years. From the sound of things, he participated in everything school had to offer him.

He played football, basketball, and baseball all while earning a 4.0 grade point average. He was prom king and salutatorian. All of this while working on the farm early in the morning before his school day had even started.

On the surface, it seems life has been easy for him, but if you listen closely, it's clear he's made his own destiny with hard work, dedication, and a positive attitude.

Reading that last sentence back does sound like I'm describing Rachel Hollis or some other motivational speaker and not a backward ball cap-wearing, smart-ass, small-town farm boy, doesn't it?

Every day I spend time with him assures me there is much more to him than meets the eye, and I can't wait to find out what I'll learn about him next.

CHAPTER 11

Mason

Dear Journal,

Miles was busy again today, but he still made time for me. I have no idea why. It's not as if I'm leaving tomorrow, but the man has set his mind on this, and there doesn't seem to be any stopping him.

I may not have asked him for a daily lesson on the history of Miles and his beloved Eastlyn, but you won't find me complaining.

Maybe he needs some sort of break or distraction from everything going on with the farm. If he needs a distraction, I'm happy to assist.

Today, I got to see the rest of town where he and all of his friends grew up. Literally.

As we drove through town, we stopped in front of each of The Crew members' homes. At first, I thought it was odd when we stopped in front of Parker's house and he began telling me all about Parker and his family, but he did this for all six of them.

Why? Because they're his family.

I have no idea what he is going to do when Rachel and Reece leave for Africa and Emmett moves to LA to be with Josh. Poor guy.

There were two stops today that I'm not sure I can even put into words, but I'll try.

In the middle of our curbside lessons, we made a stop I hadn't anticipated.

His parents' home.

Not the home they used to live in on the farm. No, we stopped at the home they currently live in.

The home they were inside when we pulled into the driveway.

When he announced where we were and that he wanted to "pop in and say hello," I broke out in a cold sweat and stopped breathing before the word hello was out of his mouth. Not fazed by the fear he had to have seen blanketing my face, he got out of the truck, behaving as though it was no big deal. Like we were running to the corner store for milk or something.

This stop certainly wasn't going to be like any of the other lessons we'd had so far, at least not to me. I sat there glued to my seat, staring out the windshield.

When he opened my door, he confessed that he'd told them all about the fancy writer staying in their humble little town, and they'd made him promise to bring her by.

So there we were.

When I didn't show any intentions of getting out of the truck, he leaned in front of me and unbuckled my seat belt, and in true Miles Montgomery fashion, he stopped two inches from my face and said just the right thing.

"Don't be scared, City Mouse. They don't bite. They just want to meet the person who has me so distracted."

When I didn't reply, he said, "Don't worry, they're gonna love you. It'd be impossible not to."

Yes, journal... He. Said. That!

And I forgot to mention that he turned his baseball cap around before he leaned in. Damn him and his backwards hat and silky smooth words. He may be keeping his hands to himself, but sometimes, in moments like these, it feels as intimate as I'm sure it would if his hands caressed my body the way I dream they do every night.

His sweetness had me so high I swear I floated out of that truck and right through the front door of his parents' home.

It turns out, Mitch and Krista Montgomery are the sweetest people and could not have been more welcoming. Their home was the newest I'd seen in town and even had a pool out back. They may not live like the rest of the folks in Eastlyn but humble doesn't even begin to describe them.

Mitch is a big man with a gruff voice, but from what I could tell, he was nothing but a great big teddy bear, especially when you bring up his son. It was evident that Miles and Mitch are extremely close, and more than anything, it's obvious his dad is incredibly proud of him.

Krista is the same and gushed at the thought of their daughter who was due in just a few months. She made sure to walk me down the hallway lined with photos of Miles and his sister, Stacci, from the time they were babies to last year's holiday photo of everyone.

It's obvious his sister is missed and they wish they were closer to their grandson and soon-to-arrive granddaughter.

Miles takes after his dad, and his sister is the spitting image of their mom. They are a beautiful family.

We didn't stay long since they had another meeting later that afternoon, but the Montgomerys couldn't have been more welcoming. Even though he'd said what he said in the truck, it didn't feel like I was meeting a new boyfriend's parents. It all just felt, I don't know...normal.

They asked questions about my writing, and I even gave his mom my pen name. She said she was going to look Eve Villanelle up online, and I turned a hundred shades of pink at the thought of his mom reading the steamy bits.

Journal, I guess I'm not completely done caring what people think, after all. Well, at least when it comes to Miles's mom. She matters for reasons I'm not ready to put on paper just yet.

Once we were back in the truck, he didn't bring up his parents anymore. He acted like it was no big deal at all. Perfectly normal.

Where he took me next was just as special to him.

A couple miles out of town, there was a tiny little house with a long dirt road on the side of a piece of property that leads to a huge open field. This wasn't just any field, though. It was alive with green grass and littered with little purple flowers. Big pine trees that seemed to go on forever grew on the far end of the field.

We left the truck on the edge of the grass and went for a walk that eventually landed us at a huge fire pit. This is where Miles and The Crew spent their time growing up. The house near the road that led us here belongs to his friend Reece's grandparents so they always had access. Apparently, deep in the trees there were natural and teenage made spots that were perfect for jumping their bikes, so eventually they just called their happy place, The Jumps.

He described it all in such detail that I could hear the distant echo of their laughter over the crackling roar of a bonfire.

He wasn't just showing me Eastlyn. He was showing some of what made him the man he is today.

He was showing me his heart.

And I like what I see.

All of it.

I already had it bad after that sunrise and my day at the farm, but after today, I'm a goner.

CHAPTER 12

Mason

Oh, Journal, what am I going to do? Miles is slowly (like painfully slowly) but surely wooing me.

Like old-school wooing.

I can see the exhaustion on his face from his crazy-busy schedule, yet he keeps finding time for me every day. Today, he only had an hour to spare, but he still made it happen. And it was by far the best hour of my day.

We went to Tom's Drive-in and had strawberry milkshakes. Lou sat at our feet while we devoured the sweet treats grinning at each other like idiots.

We sat at a little picnic bench outside a red-roofed walk-up-only burger joint and stared at each other while slurping the sugary bliss through our straws. We didn't say much. Couldn't really as those milkshakes were thick as molasses.

It was like living out a scene from a movie where the two star-crossed lovers each have a straw in the milkshake and smile at each *other as their faces come close together. The only difference is neither of us like each other enough to share a milkshake. I mean, that's next level relationship stuff right there.*

Journal, I really want to get to that kind of next level with him, but I'm only here for a little while, and my life is in New York. Nothing can come of this. No matter how good it feels or how badly I want him, in the end, Miles and I simply don't work.

If only that weren't the case.

Miles was acting so dang dreamy there was a moment when I was thinking how much like a movie this seemed, and I actually giggled out loud. His mouth was occupied and spared me from all his usual silly comments, but it doesn't mean his eyes didn't speak a thousand words while his eyebrows asked a million questions.

There was no hiding from his eyes, and his what's so funny look makes me giggle all over again.

After days of nonstop talking—granted, mostly on his side—it was interesting how compatible things continued to feel even when we weren't in deep conversation. It was one of the best hours I've ever spent, and all we did was drink strawberry shakes.

Yes, out of all the flavors Tom's offers, we both got strawberry because well, it's our favorite. What can I say? We both have great taste.

He dropped me off today like he has every day with a peck on the cheek after walking me to the front door.

Always leaving me wanting more.

He's no fool. He knows exactly what he's doing.

Even though he leaves me pining for more, he and the entire town are also providing piles of inspiration, and I'm writing at a ferocious pace.

I decided to go to The Jury Room for dinner, and that's where I ran into Emmett and Rachel. When they told me that Ken, the foreman at the farm, had welcomed a son earlier in the week and that Miles was working around the clock so he could take time off to be with his family, I fell ever harder.

I knew he had meetings, knew things were crazy with harvest season in full swing, but I had no idea the small blocks of time he's been taking off to spend with me were his only breaks.

Miles Montgomery is turning out to be quite special. Like one of my leading men come to life. However, most of my characters also have that one big fatal flaw that gets in the way of everything and causes heartbreak for my heroines.

If I let Miles write our story, will I be left at some point trying to mend my own broken heart?

Will my life imitate art?

CHAPTER 13

Mason

Dear Journal,

MILES MONTGOMERY HAS ME HOOK, *line, and sinker.*

I'm done!

Waving the white flag.

I surrender.

No man has ever made such a sincere effort to get to know me.

To spend time with me.

To keep his promise and to make my day. Every. Single. Day.

Late last night, I got a text from him telling me not to plan any of my meals for today and that he hoped I didn't mind an early morning breakfast.

Needless to say, I didn't sleep at all. My mind was too preoccupied with what my day would consist of and who would be picking me up for a sunrise breakfast. He said not to worry about getting dressed, and that we wouldn't be going anywhere. I thought he must have been bringing coffee and donuts, which would have been fine by me, but of course, he surprised me yet again.

He arrived with Lou at his feet and a grocery bag under his arm. When he read my shirt that said Just One More Chapter on it, he said he liked it, but my Romance Writers Do It Better was his favorite. He loved that his comment made me roll my eyes because this means he had the effect he intended to, and the victory was all his.

Getting under my skin seems to be his thing.

Journal, the thing is, I like getting under his skin too. I love that he noticed my shirt. And I really love that he loves making me roll my eyes.

While I sat at the kitchen table, as instructed, he proceeded to make us pancakes. Amazing pancakes. Even Lou got one, hold the butter and syrup, of course.

After a quick thirty minutes, they were gone. Only the smell of pancakes and the burn of his kiss on my cheek left behind.

At noon, he was back, and this time we went to his parents' house.

Yep, you read that right, Journal, his parents' house.

Again.

His mom had lunch waiting for us, and we had a nice easygoing meal complete with her famous potato salad.

When we first walked in, I was anxious, wondering how exactly this was going to go, but it only took two minutes before I was relaxed and piling food on my plate. There were no funny looks from Mitch or Krista to make me feel like I was the new woman in their son's life.

They talked to me as though they had known me for years, asking me to grab the iced tea out of the fridge and bring it to the table. They were warm and friendly and, just like my pancakes from this morning, amazing.

They talked about how harvest was going, Ken's brand new baby boy, and argued over why Krista couldn't give Lou his own sandwich.

On the way home when I told him how sweet I thought it was that he was making Ken take time off to be with his family, he said he didn't mind covering for him at all but that he hated that it meant he got less time to take me on my tour. I told him that was sweet too, but I did understand, and I didn't need him to show me around every day if he didn't have time.

I swear if we had been acting out a scene in a film, the music would have soared and the heroine would have touched her hand to her heart going all gaga because his reply was epic.

"You may not need to see me every day, but I sure as hell need to see you every day. Time with you has become a necessity."

He needed to see me every day.

Being with me was a necessity.

For real.

That is what he said.

I keep wondering if I am having delusions of grandeur or if I'm actually just having the longest, best dream ever?

But when his lips linger on my cheek a little longer than usual when he says goodbye and the feel of his hand on the small of my back gently pushes our bodies against each other, he all but confirms I'm not out of mind just yet.

I am awake and not living in a perpetual dream state.

Only this feels better than a dream ever could.

For the rest of the afternoon, I was useless. I didn't get anything done, knowing I was going to see him six hours later.

I tried, I really did.

I went for a walk, then tried to write but ended up doing some online shopping instead. Every outfit I brought with me to Oregon had been tried on while I prepared to see him for dinner. In the end, I went with a pale pink floral maxi dress. I felt good in it, and it's important I feel good in my own skin around him because one thing I know for certain is that my insides will be off-kilter all night.

After putzing around Katie's place for what feels like days, my nerves that were balancing on the edge of combustion all day have me jumping out of my skin when the roar of his diesel engine shakes the house. The knowledge of his arrival caused my already overexcited heart to do a flip in anticipation.

Journal, you know I wanted to run to the door and tear it open, but I waited for him to knock. I didn't even let myself look out the window to take a peek, but I sure wish I had because I would have had a second or two to prepare myself. If I had, I wouldn't have audibly gasped when I pulled the door open.

The embarrassment of my gasp was well worth it when he gifted me with one of his smiles that said he knew I liked what I saw, and knowing this seemed to make him feel as good as I did.

It was only the second time I had seen him without a hat, and it was like looking at a different person. Just as devastatingly handsome but a more sophisticated version with a short hairstyle that appeared to have just enough product in it to give it a little lift and style. A short-sleeved black button-down was tucked into tight dark jeans, and Miles being Miles, he still had on his work boots. And to top it off, from behind his back came a small bunch of wildflowers.

All it took was a couple minor changes to his wardrobe, and he went from hot farm boy to...well, to sexy farm boy.

He told me I looked beautiful, and when I asked where we were going, he said my real date was waiting for him at his place. I had no idea what in the world he was talking about, but it turns out, we were both dressed up to have dinner at his house.

Before I was even out of the car, Lou was next to my door, waiting to greet me, and it was then I realized this was the date Miles was referring to. Lou had on the cutest little plaid bow tie, and I was proud to call him my date for the evening. Miles and Lou are two of the sweetest boys I've ever met.

His house was newer, on a beautiful piece of land with the nearest neighbors out of shouting distance. It wasn't too big, but it was designed to perfection from the landscaping out front to the gray paint color and white shiplap on the walls.

The dining room looked like it had never been used, but this evening, it was adorned with a larger bouquet of the same flowers he *gave me when he picked me up, as well as a meal that had to have taken all day to prepare.*

When I questioned him about how he possibly had time to do all of this, he admitted Amelia had been his accomplice, and that she left right before we got there.

Dinner was great, and as always, he was a complete gentleman, but it was clear he was exhausted. When he asked if I wanted a second glass of wine, I told him what a great time I had, but that I thought he should take me home so he could get some rest.

I don't think an early evening was in his plans, but he didn't fight my suggestion. He's clearly been burning the candle at both ends.

Tonight when he dropped me off, he gave me his usual peck on the cheek I've come to expect, and then he asked me if he could have me all day Saturday. He's taking the weekend off, and he'd like to spend it with me.

There isn't anything else I can think of that would make me happier was my reply. His tired eyes lit up, and he told me to dress casually and hoped I had sweet dreams.

Not sure how my dreams could be any sweeter than my real life unless they included Miles with his clothes off.

Now, that would be some sweet, sweet dreaming.

CHAPTER 14

Mason

Dear Journal,

MILES HAD WARNED me last night that today would be especially busy and that the only break in his schedule was his standing third Friday of the month haircut at Mel's Barber Shop. But more importantly he said after seeing me every day this week, there was no way he could go an entire day without doing so.

He swung by to pick me up, and he took me with him to get his haircut. Yes, you read that right. He wanted to see me so badly he picked me up just to go get his haircut with him.

According to Miles, no tour of Eastlyn was complete without a trip to Mel's anyway.

I kind of wish I had never gone to Mel's.

Because then I wouldn't have been sure this was more than lust and that I was actually falling in love with my tour guide.

Not only him, but the whole damn town.

Journal, I know it makes no sense that a trip to the barbershop would be the catalyst for such a declaration, but it's true.

I'll never forget the scent of spicy cologne, the low buzz of the clippers, and the dust particles floating through the beam of sunlight piercing through the shop for as long as I live.

The mutual respect and friendship Mel and the other retired old-timers at the shop had for one another was incredibly endearing. Not to mention the hysterical stories. Stories that may have only been half true but who cares when they're about Miles in his youth.

There is no doubt Miles, Montgomery Farms, and his entire family are a big piece of the heart and soul of this community. There are pictures of Miles and the farm on the wall as well as the team photo from the years when his high school baseball team won the state title. And of course, an EBC sign in the middle of it all.

This tiny barbershop sitting smack dab in the middle of Main Street is a living museum of all of the things that make Eastlyn well, Eastlyn. Nobody talked about the pictures on the wall or bragged on Miles. The men in the shop just went about their day and continued arguing over who the Trail Blazers should have drafted a couple of months ago.

While I was spinning in the empty chair next to Miles, giggling at the entertainment Mel and the other Eastlyners were providing, the bell above the door rang and in walked Miles twenty-five years from now. Mitch Montgomery may have a couple of inches and a few pounds on his son, but they are a matching set otherwise.

Mitch's presence filled the small shop instantly. Once he joined the conversation, my pulse began to pound in my ears the moment it hit me. I was falling for a man I could never be with. Forget the fact I had vowed to never fall for a man like him again because this is the least of my worries. The real problem is that as great as he may be, I am still a city mouse who is only here for a short time, and it's clear that nothing and no one could ever take Miles Montgomery away from here. And frankly, who would want to?

Journal, I am tumbling ass over teakettle downhill at top speed for this man. I know it's gonna hurt, and I know he's the kind of man who will ruin me for all men to come after him, but I feel helpless to fight the pull of him.

Instead of fighting it, I'm going to soak up these hot summer days as long as he keeps asking me to. Whether it be thirty minutes in a barbershop or watching the sunrise over his farm. Whatever little bit he can give me, I will greedily take because Miles Montgomery is everything, and you don't walk away from everything.

At least not until you walk down the jetway to the plane that will take you away from him. And that's still nine weeks away.

I'll worry about those tears once the plane doors close behind me.

CHAPTER 15

Miles

"What did you two do today?" I hear Emmett ask Mason from behind me while Josh and I prep the fire.

It's nice to have our sexiest man alive home from Los Angeles. Since Josh became a giant superstar, we don't get to see him nearly enough. But I ain't gonna lie, I'm totally tuning Mr. Hollywood out while he talks to me about the lifestyles of the rich and famous to hear Mason's answer.

"Oh, Emmett, we had so much fun."

Damn straight we did.

"We just hung out all day. He's been showing me around town and helping me research the whole small-town vibe. I have to say I love Eastlyn. It's just what I needed."

"I totally get it. I'm so glad that I'll have Eastlyn to come home to once I move to LA, but ugh, I do not want to talk about that. Tell me, what's been your favorite thing about Eastlyn so far?"

Yes, do tell...

"Well, I know it's crazy, but I love getting shakes at Tom's diner. Today was the second time we've gone to Tom's, and there is just something about it. There was this whole nostalgic feel to the day. I'm not sure if it's because he picked me up in the same old truck he drove in high school, and we spent the day driving around town, dipping our toes in the river, slurping shakes at Tom's and then finishing here at The Jumps, but I feel like I might have gotten a glimpse of what a summer day must have been like for you guys as kids. But Tom's had to be my favorite part of the day. I don't know, there is certainly something to be said about sitting across from a cute boy while we both sip on our shakes. It's just kind of dreamy."

"Dreamy? Miles Montgomery dreamy?"

Emmett's sure to say this loud enough for me to hear, and if she thinks she's giving me a hard time, she's doing just the opposite, because goddamn if it doesn't feel good to hear. Not just the dreamy part but hearing her describe the day in exactly the way I had hoped she would experience it.

Hell, yes!

"Emmy, you've known that since we were in elementary school. You've just never been brave enough to say it out loud, like Mase," I say over my shoulder.

"No, I knew you were an idiot back then, and you still are. You must have dropped something in her milkshake because I know Mason is too smart to fall for the likes of you."

"But they were strawberry, Emmett. Have you had a strawberry milkshake from Tom's? I mean, if that isn't the way to a girl's heart, I don't know what is." I look over my shoulder, and she's looking right at me with a shit-eating grin on her face. "Besides, he's kinda cute."

Could this day get any better?

"Okay, you can take it from here, Josh," I say, handing over the reins of the fire so I can get up to be next to my girl. "That is, unless you're afraid to get your pretty little Hollywood manicure dirty."

"Fuck off, Miles."

"Hey, you're the one who moved to the glitz and glamour of Southern California so you could spend your days gallivanting around the world on private planes. You trying to say you can take the boy out of Eastlyn, but you can't take Eastlyn out of the boy?"

"Damn straight. Besides, you know I've always been the fire master around here. Now go woo the poor girl."

Josh gives me a nod, and I see the guy I grew up with. "Hey, man, it's really good to have you home." I pull the Oscar winner into a bro hug. "I miss you, man."

"Miss you too, asshole. The truth is, I miss this place more than I ever thought I would."

"There's no place like home," I say, stepping away from him and in Mason's direction.

My heart swells to see Mason's beaming face in the firelight as she talks to one of my best friends as if she's already one of us. A couple of steps toward her and my heartbeat is just about to find its rhythm again but wouldn't you know it falters when those dark eyes and bright smile hit me.

I'll be damned if laying her eyes on me doesn't somehow cause her smile to grow even bigger.

And that feels good.

Emmett, never one to let an opportunity to razz me pass her by, tries to ruin the moment, but try as she might, it's not possible.

"Aw, there's our dreamy milkshake spiker. So, tell me…do you two share one milkshake and drink it from two straws like in the olden days, or did he spring for two so you could have your own?"

"Emmett, I said he was kinda cute, I didn't say I would share my milkshake with him. Let's not go crazy."

She's talking to Emmett, but her gaze is still all mine.

The bonfire begins to roar, and the light from the flames adds a warm glow to her face. The way she's looking at me right now, her eyes are burning as hot as the embers at the bottom of the roaring bonfire behind me.

In fact, amid all the burning hot lust simmering between us, there's also a sense of comfort. Like I've known her my entire life. Seeing her here with The Crew feels right. Josh, Emmett, Amelia, Reece, and Rachel are all here. If only Parker and Audrey were here, the night would be perfect.

Ending this perfect day with perfect people and my perfect city mouse feels not only right but so very good.

She's the one.

And I'm fucking scared shitless.

I always knew she was out there.

Now she's here, and I'd do anything not to fuck up what we already have. I made sure to work my ass off all week long so I'd have this weekend with her. If I stop moving, I may pass out from exhaustion, but it was worth it.

As if reading my mind and wanting me to know the work was worth it, Mason closes the small distance between us. She lifts up on her toes and kisses me.

Really kisses me.

Right here.

In front of everyone.

The pressure of her hands on my shoulders to keep her balance is all it takes for me to take the moment a little caveman, lifting her up so her legs wrap around my waist. I walk her backward placing her on my open tailgate where we continue our kiss for all to see.

She tastes a little like the spearmint of her gum and a whole hell of a lot like heaven.

There's a faint buzz of activity behind us. My brain knows it's the sound of everyone egging us on, but neither of us pays them any mind.

On the tailgate, she's sitting higher than me and continuing to take what she wants. Leaning down, she holds my face, taking the lead again. I'm new to taking it slow, but if this is what it gets me, I'll keep it up as long as it takes.

Having the confirmation that she reciprocates my feelings means more than getting in her pants, and I'm certainly not going to put on the brakes because my friends are watching.

Eventually, she comes up for air, and with her forehead against mine, I feel her minty breath across my face when she whispers, "Thanks for a great week. I really enjoyed my tour." She punctuates her gratitude with a giggle. Shadowing her, I cup her face in my hands and give her one more peck on the lips.

I could kiss her all night.

I know we are grown-ass people, but I feel like a teenager who finally figured out how this whole making-out thing really works.

The taunting of my so-called friends finally registers.

Doing a little spin, I take a bow and then settle myself between Mason's legs.

It kills me to have my back to her, but I've committed her firelit glow to memory. Her long honey-colored hair is up in a high ponytail that emphasizes her slender neck. I was glad she left it up when she changed out of her simple white T-shirt and her cutoffs that fit her just right but not in that Daisy Duke kind of way. They were appropriate *and* still hot as hell, but she insisted on changing into the light flowy dress she has on right now. She went from the girl next door pretty, to sexy and flirty in her little summer dress that make her legs look a mile long. Currently, everything but her legs is hidden by my flannel and the loose material of her dress falling just right over her thighs to keep her modest.

The flannel she put on when the temperature dropped. She didn't ask, and I didn't offer. The shirt was on the passenger seat when she got in the truck earlier today, and she just put it on. I did bring it for her, just in case she needed it, but I didn't tell her that. She saw it and simply put it on of her own accord. I love that she felt comfortable enough to perform this small act without asking.

I'm never washing the damn thing ever again.

Having my back to her is also okay because her arms are wrapped around my neck and mine are resting on her silky-smooth legs.

In the middle of a debate about men's bedazzled jean pockets —I firmly believe they're jeans not chandeliers and do not need to be adorned with anything remotely close to bedazzling—her lips gently graze the shell of my ear, and I can't for the life of me figure out why I feel like I need to stick around. All I want to do is throw her in the cab of my truck and take her home and of course straight to bed, but I restrain my testosterone-laced wants and chill.

Mason O'Brien is not a one-night stand. Time with her is not something you rush. She is a fine wine you savor, and when we do finally sleep together, I plan on doing just that. Savoring the hell out of her.

I catch a glimpse of Reece, and he gives me a barely there nod that says he sees it too. She finally found me, and he's happy for me.

There's no way he could be as happy for me as I am for him and Rachel. To see them back together is something I've hoped would happen for the past ten years. It may have taken twelve hours stuck alone in an elevator, but all that matters is that twelve hours brought them back together. And now with Mason by my side, all is right in the world.

Well, almost. I still don't understand why Emmett and Josh are engaged. I mean, I get they're best friends who made a pact when they were kids, but that doesn't mean you actually get married. Watching them in the same firelight illuminating the love between Reece and Rachel, I don't see anything but friends with a capital F.

We all know Josh isn't into Emmy that way; he never has been. I have a feeling this is all for the press and to advance his career in some way, and I don't like it at all. Especially when it means Emmett will be moving away right after Rachel leaves with Reese. Our little group keeps spreading its wings, and as happy as I am for everyone, it kills me every time someone moves away, even if only for six months but especially when I don't think it's for the right reasons.

Josh has always been the selfish one of the group. In the past, it was just something we gave him shit about, but now Emmett is involved. If this ends in heartbreak and humiliation for her, it will be a different story, and he'll have all of us to answer to. Once I get two seconds alone with him, I need to make sure a conversation is had.

For the next couple of hours, stories are told, sing-alongs are sung, and s'mores are eaten. All the while, Mason and I have had constant contact with one another.

Hand holding. Check.

Light back rubbing. Check

Soft caresses that are almost undetectable. Check.

Quick kisses whenever the urge takes either one of us. Check.

Since making the bold move of kissing me, she hasn't stopped touching me.

Something changed tonight, and it's pretty powerful.

So powerful, I know without a doubt now that she's mine.

I've known from the start, but I needed her to figure it out on her own, and by God, I think she has.

The night is wrapping up as Josh, Reece, and I put out what's left of the bonfire. Mason is making plans with the girls, and while the girls are distracted, I take the opportunity to talk to Josh, who's busy on his phone.

He's been preoccupied with his phone for the past five years.

"Hey, man. You've been on that thing all night. Everything okay?" I ask.

Looking like he's been busted with his hand in the cookie jar, he quickly shuts off the device and shoves it in his pocket. Hmm…

"We're rarely all together like this, but it's like you aren't really here. What gives?" Reece asks, backing me up.

"Sorry, guys, just working on something with my manager." Finally focusing on us and shaking off the fact that I called him out on what, I have no idea, but I don't believe he's working on a "deal" of any kind. "Hey, Mason's really cool, man. You seem to be really serious about her," he says, taking the conversation off him.

"Serious as a heart attack. She's it, Josh."

"What do you mean, she's it? Like she's the one?" Reece questions in a whisper when Josh stares at me speechless like I just told him I was running for president or something.

"Without a doubt."

"So what you're telling me is that Miles Montgomery, Mr. One-Night Stand, Mr. Hit It and Quit It is in love?"

Glancing over my shoulder, I make sure she's still distracted before confirming his smart-assed yet well-deserved question. "I mean, she doesn't know that, and you two are the first I've said any of this to, but yeah, I'm pretty sure that's what this is."

Wow, did I really just say that out loud?

Not gonna lie, like everything else tonight, it feels good.

"You're saying you don't want anyone else but her? Ever again? Only her?" Josh presses, clearly in disbelief.

I've been so certain of how I feel about her that I never really thought about it that way, but now, hearing him say it, I'm really taking in exactly what it means to find the one, and I couldn't be more confident about my answer.

"Yep. She's the real deal. The thought of being with anyone else makes me a little sick to my stomach, to tell you the truth."

With their eyes bugging out of their heads, Josh and Reece look at one another in disbelief.

"I'm happy for you, man. I always wondered if you'd find love, and I'm glad to be here to witness it. I feel like I miss everything these days, and I'm glad I got to meet her," Reece replies while Josh stands back examining me.

His reaction to the possibility of me finding love reminds me why I started this conversation in the first place.

"Well, you must know how I feel, Josh. You and Emmett are engaged after all."

Clearing his throat, he gives me what feels like a well-rehearsed answer. "We've known each other since we were kids. I've loved her my entire life, so there isn't that whole new exciting thing like you have with Mason. What Emmett and I have has grown over time. She's one of my best friends. No, she is my best friend."

"You, and Parker, and Reece are my best friends, but you don't see me asking any of you to marry me. What's really going on, Josh? I can't help but think there's more to this engagement than meets the eye. Please tell me this isn't something your 'people' said would be good for your image? Because I may love you like a brother, but I will also rip your balls off if you hurt her for some sort of publicity stunt. You know that, right?"

"Miles, you know I love her. I would never marry her if I thought I was going to hurt her. Besides, all that matters is that Emmett and I are on the same page. She knows what she's getting into."

Reece's forehead creases as he shakes his head and takes a step back. I've only seen him do this a hand full of times. He's angry. Really angry when he whispers his rage so the girls don't overhear, "She's knows what she's getting into? What the fuck does that mean?"

Trying to calm the situation I had no intention of starting, I jump in. "I know you love her like a sister, like family, but it's not the same as being in love with her, dude. I know I'm new to all this love stuff, but I could have told you that before Mason O'Brien walked into The Verdict and planted her ass on a stool at the bar."

"Listen, all relationships are different, and we can't all be as perfectly in love as you are. You don't need to worry about Emmett. I'll take good care of her. I promise."

This is not the answer I want to hear, but I know I'm not going to get the answer I'm looking for tonight because I can feel a different kind of fiery energy coming up behind me like a damn crackle in the air, and when the warmth of her hand clasps mine, I'm officially done talking to Josh. But we will continue this conversation before anyone walks down any aisles.

"Hey, babe, you and the girls all set?"

It may be dark out here, but the smile beaming up at me fills this man-whore's heart full to the brim.

"Yep. All set, *babe*."

Ah, so that's what has her smiling like a beacon in the night. She liked me calling her babe, and I like that she liked it.

Luckily, Rachel wraps herself around Reece, tampering down his rage, if only momentarily. Even though they were together as kids, the decade apart finds them working in sync together again like they were never apart. Watching them complete each other again balances out the group. If only we all felt the same about Josh and Emmett.

Mason tugs on my arm, and I lean down as commanded. She whispers in my ear, "Miles, please take me home."

When she pulls back, it's clear she doesn't mean she wants to go home because she's bored. No, she wants me to take her home in the biblical sense.

"Hey, man, you got this?" I say, looking over my shoulder at

Reece as I pull a giggling Mason behind me on the way to my truck.

He laughs and waves me off.

Lou is loaded in the back seat, and the truck is bouncing over the rough terrain of the field, but it's nowhere as erratic as my warring feelings.

Feelings that are new and confusing as hell.

I never thought I would tell myself I wasn't ready to sleep with a woman, but I don't want to fuck this up by moving too fast.

Even if I want her so bad my dick is about to rip through the seam of my jeans I have to use my other head this time around. It's not worth the risk of making a misstep and ruining things before they've officially begun.

Once we've passed Reece's grandparents' house that we learned in Vegas now belongs to him, we finally hit the pavement and the drive levels out. However, my brain is still moving a million miles a minute. When she finally speaks, her voice calms me.

"Thank you for a wonderful day. Your friends are really great."

"They think you're pretty spectacular, too. You know that, right? I think they like you better than me. Correction. I know they like you better than me."

She laughs. "I'm just the new kid in town. The newness will wear off, and you'll all tire of me eventually. They'll forget all about me once I'm back in New York."

"Not a chance," I say, ignoring the gut punch of her reminder that she won't be staying here forever.

"Trust me. You haven't seen the truly annoying side of me yet."

"Mason, you can try your best, but I promise you, I will never tire of you."

She turns in her seat so she has an unencumbered view of me.

"What about the annoying stuff. You really have no idea what you're dealing with."

When we reach the city limits, the streetlights illuminate the cab of the truck, and her bright eyes surprisingly look much more serious than I expected them to. She really means it. She thinks when I see all sides of her, even the ugly ones, I'll run. That she won't be enough.

God, I'd love to obliterate the asshole who made her feel less than for all of those years. Along with her family. Yes, I have a few things to say to them as well.

"Babe, I don't know how to tell you this, but you're stuck with me."

Her breath hitches, and my insides do too. I just told her she was mine—that she was the one—without really telling her any of those things, of course.

She has no idea that I've never said this to anyone. That there has never been anyone I've wanted to say it to.

When we pull up to the house I run around to let her out before I get a word out, she says, "Come on, Lou!"

She's not just inviting me in; she's inviting Lou in as well.

"You sure Katie won't mind?"

"Well, I'm not gonna let him stay in the truck all by himself until the morning."

Be still my beating heart.

This woman may like me enough to ask me to stay over, but she *loves* my dog.

She was so worth the wait.

When we reach the front door where I typically leave her with a kiss on the cheek, she unlocks the door, and then oh, so coyly says, "Thanks for the milkshake." She rises on her toes, and her lips find mine for at least the thirtieth time tonight. Only, this time, it's not an innocent peck in front of my friends. It's a full force, no-holds-barred, tongues-dancing kiss that says she wants so much more.

Lou pushes his way between our legs, a reminder we're still on the front porch and haven't even opened the door. Reaching around her, I turn the doorknob and push the door ajar, guiding us inside.

Lou runs and jumps on the overstuffed chair covered in pillows and blankets like he owns the place. I know Katie wouldn't be happy to see it.

"Lou, get down right…"

"He's fine, just leave him."

She drops her purse and my flannel at her feet and leans against the wall.

"If you say so." Her chest is heaving up and down while she waits for me against the wall. "How are you doing?"

"I'd be better if we were doing some more of what we were doing out there on the porch." Her voice is seductive, her chest moving up and down in anticipation and want.

Fuck, she's killing me right now.

I cave, unable to hold back.

Pinning her against the wall, I press my body lightly against her while my hands hold most of my weight on the wall next to her head. I leisurely kiss her exposed neck, making my way to her earlobe. It was a hot day, and the taste of salt on my lips is fucking delicious. Her hair is still up in her high ponytail, and I can smell the smoke from the fire clinging to it.

I trace the shell of her ear with my tongue. "You like that, City Mouse?"

"Yes."

"You want me, don't you, Mason?" I pull back so I can gaze into the ocean of lust-filled emotions looking back at me.

"I do."

"I knew you'd come around eventually."

"Is that so?"

"Yes, ma'am."

"Enough talking."

"I get it if you can't handle a conversation like this yet." My left hand travels down her side, gently grazing the side of her breast and causing her to catch her breath yet again. "We can talk later." My thumb finds its way across her nipple, and the silky material of her cute little summer dress leaves little to the imagination as it pebbles under my touch.

Unable to find her voice, she nods her head with her full lips parted, begging me to take them. Obligingly, I do just that, devouring her like a man starved. And she feasts on me just the same.

Our hands are all over each other.

I'm not sure how, but she feels even better than I've been imagining since I watched her walk away from me on her first night in town.

Somehow, we've made it to the couch, and as usual, she's taking the lead. I'm on my back, and she's straddling me, setting a ferocious pace as she grinds herself on me. She must not realize I've been dreaming about her every night for two weeks and it's not gonna take much more before I blow.

"Babe, let's take this to your bed."

Her smile spreading against my lips tells me she's been having similar dreams. She wastes no time getting off me, then takes me by the hand to help me up and follow her to the back of the house.

When we get to her room, she turns on the little lamp next to the bed. Slipping the tiny spaghetti straps off her shoulders, she lets her dress fall to her feet, and hand to God, I've never seen anything so beautiful. Her skin is flawless, her breasts are full and natural and her pert pink nipples are begging for my mouth. The sexy curve of her hips is alluring with her thumbs in the thin sides of her panties as she teases me with the promise of baring herself to me completely. Of course I want to see all of her, but if I don't stop her right this second, things are going to go farther than I'm ready for them to go. I still haven't shown her everything, and I'm not taking her completely until I do.

Closing the space between us, I pick her up and gently toss her on the bed. When she sees me kick off my shoes, she props herself up on her elbows to watch me. Wearing nothing but her panties, she looks like a wet dream.

After I pull my T-shirt over my head, she catcalls me like I'm a stripper.

"Take it off!"

I throw my shirt at her, and she makes a show of taking a big whiff of it.

"Yum…campfire."

The gleam in her eyes, the glow in her cheeks, the want in her voice, and the way she can't stop moving her closed legs together tell me she's ready. She wants it all.

When I pull down my shorts, her eyes grow big and her mouth agape in anticipation. When I don't pull down my briefs, she looks disappointed, and it's adorable. I join her on the bed, and when my hand touches her soft skin and starts to explore her body, the simple act has her writhing and moaning for more.

I can't take my eyes off her face, so when she opens her heavy lids and looks at me, there's an unmistakable connection.

A mutual feeling.

Something more than just going to bed with the hot tourist from New York.

When I look into her eyes, I feel a realness I've never felt with another woman.

I'm looking at my future.

My family.

My happy ending and not the kind of happy ending I'm usually looking for.

"Thank you for inviting me in tonight."

She nods.

"I hope you aren't disappointed," I say as I pull her nipple between my lips.

Her back arches, and her eyes close again. "How could I be?" she asks in a lust-filled sigh.

Because I can't give you what you want.
Not yet.

CHAPTER 16

Mason

The whirring of activity in the kitchen stirs me awake, my body stretching along with the smile spreading across my face. I'm used to finding myself alone in my bed each morning, but I was so looking forward to waking up in Miles' arms.

Clank...clank...clank.

Tap...tap...tap.

Ah, the sounds of Sweet Lou's dog tag clanking against his collar while his toenails tap on the hardwood floors. Miles may not be in my bed, but both of the boys are still here. I can't think of a better way to wake up. Well, Miles on the pillow next to me wouldn't be so bad either.

Stretching my arms above my head, I arch my back on a lazy yawn when the rich smell of fresh coffee brewing hits my senses. As if the morning wasn't looking bright already, knowing Miles is the kitchen making himself at home has my smile growing to the point of painful.

He didn't leave.

He also didn't "sleep" with me.

Eastlyn isn't forever, but for right now, it's pretty great.

I'm happy.

Because of him.

I can think of one thing that would make me a bit happier, but he did give plenty.

Flashes of last night zip through my head like a kaleidoscope of pleasure.

The memory of his gentle caresses mixed with flicks of his tongue and everything else he did with his hands led to more pleasure than I can ever remember having in one night.

I'm afraid I'm going to get used to the way he makes me feel, and then I'll be back to sleeping alone in a matter of weeks.

But for now, I'm here, in Eastlyn, and I deserve to feel good.

To be happy.

Enough lying around. He stayed over, and he's apparently made coffee, and I do believe I smell bacon sizzling on the stove. That bacon has to be one of two reasons the toenails of a certain German shepherd are tap-dancing on the wood floors in the kitchen. That and the presence of his daddy. Last night, he made me want to do a little dance or two too.

I throw on my robe and tiptoe to the bathroom, praying I get there to brush my teeth and clean up before I say good morning.

When I reach the safety of the bathroom, I quickly pile my hair on top of my head in a messy bun that doesn't look much better than the mess that was hanging down my back, but it's my go-to, and I might as well keep it real. I can barely brush my teeth through the smile looking back at me in the mirror.

Trying to sneak into the kitchen is next to impossible with Lou around. He's waiting for me in the hallway when I step out of the bathroom, and before I've even rounded the corner to the kitchen, Miles is greeting me.

"Morning, babe!" he yells from the stove.

God, I love when he calls me that.

Hi, my name is Mason, I'm thirty-three years old and still feel like a teenager when the guy I'm crushing on calls me babe.

"Morning. You're up early."

And you don't have a shirt on.

More flashes of last night bounce around my head, and my fingers tingle remembering the feel of his skin on my fingertips after touching every inch of him I could reach last night.

"Yeah, sorry about that. It's one of the many drawbacks of having sleepovers with a farmer. Or someone who grew up in the life anyway." He smiles that charming smile of his and flips a sizzling piece of bacon in the pan.

"As long as I get the sleepovers, I'm pretty sure I can handle the early mornings."

Shaking his head with a chuckle, he turns the dial on the stove and rests his spatula on the counter. Before I know what's happening, he marches right toward me and kisses me with a furious passion.

He's taking possession of me, and I want him to possess me.

Every piece of me.

I've written about my characters feeling this way, but I don't think I've ever actually felt it myself. I get it now, only it's a stronger emotion than I really ever knew.

I don't even blink when his hands grab my backside so he can lift me on the counter to intensify our connection. Our hands are all over each other just like they were last night.

I've fallen under his spell.

There's no way he's feeling what I'm feeling, right?

I'm sure he has sleepovers all the time. Mornings after are more than likely the norm for him.

But then again, we didn't have sex, so is this really a morning after?

Does he do this for the women he hasn't slept with?

Why *didn't* we have sex?

Technically, Katie was right. He did get in my panties, but I think she would be surprised to learn the deed wasn't actually done.

Gah! Why am I in my head asking myself a million questions when his lips are on mine?

Just as I focus on his lips, he pulls them from mine, holding my face in his rough hands and leans his forehead against mine.

"You can have as many sleepovers as you want, City Mouse."

Great, now I'm thinking how many sleepovers he's had and with how many different women he's had them with. Yuck.

He lifts an eyebrow and tilts his head, curious why I've had a sudden change of mood, but he doesn't push.

"You stay there. I have to finish breakfast."

"I can help."

"No way, I want to feed you."

Before he turns the stove back on, he pours me a cup of coffee. "Milk and sugar?"

"Yes, please."

He makes my coffee with almost as much of the finesse he puts into the kiss he burns onto my cheek when he hands me my cup and gets back to his cooking.

As I watch him back at the stovetop, his pace seems a bit frantic. He's fumbling with the spatula as he tries to flip the contents of his pan, whereas minutes ago, he was sure-handed and seemed to know exactly what he was doing.

I sure hope my anxiousness hasn't rubbed off on him. If it has, it's my responsibility to make him feel better.

"So whatcha making?" I offer from my perch on the counter. "You sure I can't help with anything?"

He looks up from the stove, and his eyes are trying to tell me so many things, but I have no idea what.

"No, I have this." He turns, making himself at home. Taking eggs out of the fridge, he places the carton on the counter, opens it, and then just stares at it for a beat, searching for what's next, and I'm wondering the same.

What exactly is next?

"Over easy okay?"

"Perfect."

"Great." He turns and pushes the switch on the toaster before returning to the eggs.

This is when he starts talking at a furious pace.

"Listen, I have to be honest with you, Mason."

Here it comes.

He's going to tell me he's really into me, but he just doesn't do the commitment thing, and I'll pretend it's no big deal since I'm leaving soon, and I'm fine with just having some fun.

I should have known better.

If you listen closely to the silence between his sentences, you can hear a faint hissing sound. This would be the sound of my heart deflating. I should be telling myself I didn't want this to begin with. I've been with his type before, and it's better to get it over with now.

I hop off the counter and take a seat at the kitchen table. Feeling a bit more grounded may serve me better.

Miles releases the giant breath he'd been holding.

Here we go.

"I've slept with a lot of women."

Not what I expected.

"So I've heard."

He tilts his head with a grin. "Like I've said…I've slept with a lot of women, and here I am still single. I want to get this right, and that's why I'm going about things…well, you, differently."

He runs his hands through his unruly blond waves, almost as messy as my insides are feeling.

"Shit, I don't even know what I'm saying. This is a first for me, Mase. I've wanted to feel this and wondered when it would happen." He glances up at me and takes another deep breath and then focuses back on the stove. "I know you were expecting more last night, and babe, you have to believe me when I say I wanted to give it to you. But, dammit, Mason. I. Will. Get. This. Right."

He flips the eggs, and my insides do the same.

"I know you're here to write your book, and I know I'm not your typical reader base, but I'm pretty sure most of your stories have a happy ending, am I right?"

Stunned silent, all I can do is nod.

"Well, I want to be sure we have our happy ending too." He plates our food and joins me at the table, setting our meals in front of each of us.

I certainly don't want to offend him, but there's no way I can eat right now. My hands are shaking while my insides quiver in excitement and anticipation.

"Mason, I've been waiting thirty years for you to find me. And thank God, you finally have. You took your time, but you're here. I've been happily playing your tour guide, and yes, I wanted to show you around town and make you fall in love with Eastlyn, but more importantly, I wanted to show you me. I need you to know everything about me, Mason, and that's why we need to wait until I've shown you everything there is to know about me. I know you've heard what everyone around town says about me. You know…charming, the ladies love me, and I'm a beast between the sheets. Of course, it's all true, I mean look at me, there's nothing I can do about it."

"You're an idiot."

He's not. He's only adding humor to lighten the mood. Like the girls said at the shop my first week here, Miles is always the person to take care of everyone else. To make sure everyone feels comfortable.

"Also true." Reaching across the table and touching his fingertips with mine, he continues with another heart-stopping statement. "Not sure if you've caught on or not, but the thing is...I'm your idiot."

"You are?" I ask around my heart, which is currently stuck in my throat.

"I'm afraid you've been stuck with me since night one. Mason, you were mine the moment you walked into The Verdict. You may not have known it, but I sure as hell did."

"You did?"

"I did."

"How?"

"It's the crackle. There's no denying it."

"The crackle?"

"You heard me right. You know that thing that fills the air when we're both in the same room. You might call it a buzz or some sort of an energy, but there's no way you can deny it. In my head, I've been calling it the crackle."

"You've named it?"

"Don't feel bad that I named it before you had a chance to. Now eat and later, we'll take a little field trip. I have one last thing to share with you."

CHAPTER 17

Miles

This morning has been a cluster.

I'm off my game and all spun up for some reason.

I spent breakfast stammering over myself and talking a mile a minute like a virginal teenager asking a girl to go steady for the first time.

What was I thinking telling her about the crackle?

I've gone mad.

Now I'm sitting in my truck outside her place bracing myself for what? I have no idea.

One thing I do know is I'm scared shitless of the impact Mason has on me without even trying. Does she have any clue she holds my future in her hands?

I left her a little over an hour ago so she could get ready for the day, and I could switch trucks, feed Lou, and take a shower. Enduring a night under the sheets with Mason but not actually sealing the deal left me no option but to take care of myself in the shower. I'd had a semi since she kissed me at The Jumps, and even after yanking my own chain in the shower, nothing has changed. I have a permanent semi, and my heart feels like it's going to beat out of my damn chest.

This damn woman is something else.

Never known anyone like her.

And she wants me.

A simple farm boy from Oregon.

It's stupid to be stressed about today. To most women, it would be the piece of me that attracts them to begin with. It's something I'm proud of, but to some, it becomes all they see.

I've purposely waited as long as I could for today. Not because I'm playing games, but because I needed to know she saw me. For me. And I'd say she made it perfectly clear last night that this local farm boy was more than enough for her.

I'm making this a bigger deal than it needs to be. I know this. But when it comes to my city mouse, every single thing matters. I mean, she got out of bed last night slipped on my shirt and snuck into the kitchen to put out a bowl of water for Lou and then shared half her breakfast with him this morning. She's special.

All week long, I've done my best to act casual like I'm simply showing her around town. But on the inside, I've been holding what breath she hasn't completely stolen from me already and hoping if she saw my relationships with the people in town, it would show her I'm more than the local man-whore. More than my family business. I want her to see how much this community and the farm mean to me and need her to love Eastlyn as much as I do. Praying she might just love me too.

Finally manning up, I leave the security of my truck, but before I'm close enough to knock, the door swings open, and there is an angel standing in front of me.

If I ever doubted there was a higher power out there, she would be proof of their existence.

It's as if God sent her straight from heaven, right to me.

"You are fucking beautiful."

"You like?" she asks, lifting one of her sun-kissed shoulders while acting coy because she knows she looks good.

"Babe, you know I do. What do you call this? A onesie?"

I tug on the shorts of her one-piece floral outfit, showing off her tan legs that seem to go on forever.

"Be nice. It's called a romper."

"Well, it works."

When I bend down to kiss her, she presses herself against me while she slides her hands into the pockets of my shorts like we'd been doing this for a lifetime. Like a small kiss could never be enough.

"It feels like you were gone for days. Was it really just an hour?"

There's no way she can't feel what she does to me as close as she is to me.

"I missed you too."

Feeling her smile against my lips is my new favorite thing. Okay, one of many new favorite things, but this one is near the very top.

"Ready?"

"Can't wait to see where we're going." She closes the door behind her and links our hands. "So are we about to add pages to my journal?"

"Well, I'm hoping after last night, you would have had enough to fill the one you've got going. My plan is to buy you a case of the damn things, and if all goes to plan, I'll be providing you with plenty to fill the pages with. I'd love to be the reason you have to keep buying new ones."

"You're doing a pretty good job so far."

"Glad to hear it."

I open her door, and she places a peck on my cheek on her way in the truck, branding me with her lips.

Once the truck's engine roars to life, so does the anxiousness in my belly. I take her hand in mine, pulling away from the curb, and we're off.

"Thanks for taking me out in Betsy yesterday. I mean, this truck is nice too, but Betsy has seen things. I could feel it."

God, she's perfect.

My anxiousness is being overpowered by the excitement I've had brewing as I've waited for this day. Every word, every action of hers is easing my mind, and she doesn't have a clue.

"You have no idea the things my girl, Betsy, has seen. That old truck went through it all with me growing up. I drove her to school, to the farm, to The Jumps. There were make-out sessions in the cab and chairs set up in the bed for those nights we made the trek to the nearest drive-in movie theater."

"I bet you broke some hearts in her too."

"Never intentionally, but you're right, there may have been a tear or two shed. She's also where I sought solace when I found out my grandma Mary had passed away. I wanted to be strong for my mom and would only let myself break down with Betsy. She got me through some of the hardest times of my life and some of the best."

"Well, I can see why you love her."

"Glad you like her because she's not going anywhere. That's one of the things about having a large piece of land that's nice. One of the first things I did when I bought the place was build an out-building where I could keep her nice and safe along with my other toys."

"Other toys?"

"Oh, yes. I have toys."

And what I wouldn't give to see you straddling more than one of them.

"Look at that smile. Boys and their toys." She rolls her eyes and shakes her head. "So, tell me, what have you got hidden away that's putting a smile like that on your face?"

"Nothing too fancy. Just some ATVs and my boats."

"Did you say boats? As in more than one? EBC must pay good money for those hops."

"Well, you've got to have your fishing boat for those quiet mornings on the lake with Dad and Pops. But you need the big pontoon boat for those days full of fun, sun, beer, and friends. And of course, the jet boat for skiing and wakeboarding. They each serve their own purpose."

"I see." Her fingers gently glide through my hair. "Is the fishing boat for boys only?"

"Nah, all are welcome. Why, you want to go fishing?"

"Miles, I want to experience everything that makes you tick."

And I'm done.

For the love of all that is holy, as if I hadn't already fallen so hard there is no way in hell I'm ever getting back up—wouldn't want to—she says something like that.

"Gorgeous, not sure if you've noticed, but *you* make me tick. Everything about you. You are absolutely astoundingly gorgeous, and that's not even the most interesting thing about you."

"Miles…"

"It's true. I know we've been on the Miles Montgomery tour for the past week or two, but it's because I'd do anything to spend more time with you. Every day, hell, every minute I discover something new about you that makes me want you that much more."

"What are you talking about?" she all but whispers.

"Where do I even begin? I love to hear you talk about your writing and how passionate you are about not only your process but the entire industry. I love that you don't care what other people think, and you just do your own thing. I swear you know more about beer, wine, and tequila than anyone I know, and I know people, Mason." She giggles from across the cab. "Don't even get me started on how smart you are. So much smarter than I could ever hope to be. We can talk about anything and everything. You're business savvy. You have strong opinions that are all your own and that make you who you are. I love that you love the overstuffed chair in the back corner of Brass Tacks, and when there's someone else in your spot, your lower lip pops out like a little kid. And you have awesome statement clothes that crack me up. Not to mention, you love my dog, and he loves you right back."

Taking a peek at her out of the corner of my eye, she appears dumbfounded.

I do believe I've rendered her speechless.

Good.

She needs to realize what's happening here is the real deal. I've heard enough about her leaving and this being a temporary thing.

Minutes later, we've arrived.

This is it.

"Yes! I can't believe I haven't been here yet," she says, gazing up at the Eastlyn Brewing Company sign above the large brick building. "You had me so busy with all the old-school parts of Eastlyn that I forgot all about the big tourist hot spot! Are you trying to butter me up before you show me whatever it is you still need to show me?"

"Nope, no buttering you up. Shall we?"

I walk around the truck, but she looks at me with concern wrinkling her forehead and looking adorable as she scans the nearly empty parking lot. "Miles, I don't think they're open yet. It's 10:30 on a Sunday morning."

"Come on."

Taking my hand, she slides out of the truck and follows my lead. When we reach the big black doors with a ten-foot version of the EBC logo on them, I take out my keys and open the doors.

"Uh, Miles…"

"Welcome to Eastlyn Brewing Company."

"What?"

"Come on. The team should be preparing for the lunch rush

that will start in another hour or so, and I'd like you to show you around."

"What in the world is happening right now?"

Ignoring her question, I walk us through the front doors and then lock them behind us.

Things are pretty quiet, but I can hear activity in the tasting room, and the lights are on back in the pub.

"Miles, is that your dad? Wait, is that you?"

She's spied the pictures on the wall. I stand and wait for her to connect the dots on her own.

It's obvious she wants to go back to where we first walked in, so I let go of her hand, freeing her to explore. She heads right back to the wall next to the entrance doors to read the plaques next to each picture telling the history of the company.

"Boss man, what are you doing here on a Sunday?"

"Hey, Dave, how's it going? What are you doing here on a Sunday? Everything okay?"

"I was actually leaving some paperwork for you on your desk and thought I'd help a bit before I left. Things stayed busy in the pub all week. I know you've been burning the candle at both ends, but I'm glad you're here. Not only do I need you to sign a few things but I also have an update on that investor in Portland. You have a few minutes?"

"Sure thing, but first, I'd like you to meet my girlfriend, Mason."

Her gasp is audible, even from the other side of the room. If her beaming face is any indication, I'm guessing she likes hearing me call her my girlfriend as much as I liked saying it.

"Girlfriend? Miles Montgomery, Eastlyn's, correction... Oregon's most eligible bachelor is off the market? Alert the presses but more importantly, let me meet this woman!"

Slapping him on the shoulder, I stand next to my general manager and right hand, introducing him to "my girlfriend."

"Dave Shay, meet Mason O'Brien. Mason, meet Dave, he's the

general manager here at the brewery and the man who keeps things alive and well here at the home front while I'm traveling and dealing with everything else. The place doesn't run without this man."

"Hi, Dave, it's nice to meet you." She reaches out a hand, and he takes it and covers the top of their hands with his other.

"Not as nice as it is to meet you." Not letting go of her hand, he turns his attention to me smiling his approval.

The door to the back swings open, and one of our tasting room servers walks through, sees me, and mutters, "*Shit*," under their breath and turns right back around and through the doors.

"Dave, do you mind if I steal my *boyfriend* away for a minute or two?"

"Not at all. It was nice to meet you, and when he goes back to his office to sign the contracts I left on his desk, come on back and I'll take you on a little tour."

"Will do." Her eyes land back on me, piercing me with a look that says I need to start talking.

Taking her hand back in mine, where it belongs, I don't say anything, and she seems content to wait for me to explain.

We push through the doors at the back of the tasting room that leads to where the magic happens. Her steps stutter as we pass the giant tanks full of her favorite beer, Montgomery hops, and my family's future.

It isn't fancy back here with the concrete floors, machinery, and supplies everywhere you look, but I know this is her chocolate factory. Her eyes are aglow with the light reflecting off the rows and rows of massive silver containers as if it were Christmas morning.

"I promise I'll take you on your own personal tour as soon as we have a little chat. You won't need Dave for that."

She squeals, and she and her little romper jump straight up in the air. As soon as her feet hit the ground, she schools her face, trying to remind herself she isn't happy with me.

One of the things I love about Mason is her inquisitiveness, so I know it's killing her to not ask questions while we pass all the equipment filled with one of the loves of her life.

It's Sunday, so when we reach the office, the place is empty. There are several rows of desks, a large conference room, and five offices. My office is at the end of a short hallway with Dave's office, and Dad's office on the left of the hallway, while on the right is Rhonda, our head of marketing's office, and my assistant Bennett's office.

I flip the light switch on in the room I spend more time in than I ever could have imagined. Simultaneously, I hear her read the sign on the door.

"Miles Montgomery. President and CEO."

Feeling a bit sheepish, I shove my hands in my pockets and shrug my shoulders.

"So this is why you don't work the farm anymore?"

"Yep. I do a surprisingly large amount of paperwork and travel," I say, sitting down on the couch on the far wall of the room. I don't think I've ever sat over here.

All my time is spent behind my desk. I've never really had a reason to kick back and relax. It's a nice couch.

Her arms are crossed as she leans against the doorframe. "Why keep this a secret?"

"I guess I just wanted you to know me. People can get a little distracted by the business, and I wanted you to know me first. EBC has been my heart and soul for over a decade, but it's not all that I am."

"But how did I not figure it out? Why didn't anyone say anything in all the conversations I've had about my love for EBC? I am so confused."

"Well, The Crew had specific instructions not to mention it."

"I'm sorry, what?"

Shit, she's pissed.

This may not go quite the way I had hoped it would.

"What's the big deal?"

Walking around the office examining every picture, book, or memento she comes across, she answers me but is looking at my bookshelves and not me. She's avoiding eye contact.

"The big deal is you lied to me, Miles. On top of that, you asked your friends to lie to me. I feel like an idiot."

She turns on me with fire in her eyes.

I make to stand so I can be near her, touch her, look her in her eyes and calm her because touching her will calm me. But she puts a stop to that real quick.

"Stay there."

"Yes, ma'am."

Not gonna lie. She's hot as hell all fired up like this. That doesn't mean I'm not scared shitless at the moment.

"When we were at the farm, we talked about Montgomery Farms and how you worked with EBC. You lied to me."

"Never."

"Yes you did, Miles."

"I. Did. Not. Lie. To. You. Mason."

"But you did."

"Come on, Mase. There wasn't any ill intent. Quite the opposite actually. I did it so what we have between us is authentic."

Her mouth hangs open. Appalled.

"Authentic?" Incredulous, her voice squeaks at my statement. "Since when is lying authentic? That is the most ridiculous thing I've ever heard!"

"Mason," I say calmly.

"What?" she barks.

"I never lied to you. I just didn't share all the information."

"Is there a difference?" The shrillness in her voice is gone, but still, she is nowhere near ready to relent.

"There sure the hell is a difference," I say, fighting the urge to stand from the couch and rush to her. "And if you want to be pissed because I cared enough about you, about us, to want to start things with the only two things that mattered, you and me, then so be it. I will not apologize for wanting to get this right. For wanting you to know me for me and not my money or my company. Trust me, the way you salivate over EBC, it would have been a surefire way to earn points with you, but then I would have never known if it was me or the free beer you really wanted."

She finally cracks what looks a whole lot to me like a ghost of a smile. "Free beer really would have been a distraction. I guess I can see your point there."

Thank God, I'm getting through to her.

"Exactly. Can I get up now?"

Biting her lower lip, she slowly shakes her head back and forth. And before I know, she's sauntered over to me and climbs onto my lap straddling me. When she runs her hands through my hair, her smile fades. Even with the whiplash of her emotions throwing me off balance, there's no mistaking the sincerity in her eyes.

"Did you really think I was the type of woman who would only want you for your money or I guess in your case, beer?"

"No, not really. I know you well enough to know that's not important to you, but I also needed to know that a regular old farm boy was enough for a woman like you. I mean, I know I'm a catch. Hell, I know I'm more man than you ever bargained for, but I still needed to be just me for a while, not the CEO of your favorite beer company. In the end, I'm still just a farm boy who worked hard and got lucky."

"Well, beer company or no beer company, you are more than enough, Miles Montgomery." Her lips tenderly brush against mine. "I still don't know how in the world I missed it? How did I never put it together? EBC comes up all the time. I get that you told The Crew not to mention it, but what about the rest of the town?"

"Well, it's old news around Eastlyn, and you can count on

everyone around town to do their best to keep each other humble. Let's just say there's no bragging or putting folks on a pedestal in these parts. I did think you might have figured it out at the farm. Again, I didn't lie to you that day. We do grow the hops for EBC beer. I just didn't tell you all the bits and pieces of our organization that day."

"No, you certainly did not."

"You pissed?"

"Honestly?"

"As scared shitless as I am to hear your answer, yes please."

"I was for a second. But really, I was just embarrassed. But no, I'm not mad."

"Really?"

"Really." She circles her hips on my lap. "In fact, it makes me feel all warm and fuzzy inside."

"All warm and fuzzy, huh?"

She kisses me again, and I feel the vibration of her confirmation against my lips.

"And why is that?"

She slides off my lap so she's sitting with her back against the arm of the couch and her tan legs rest across my thighs.

"Well, I'm not going to lie and say knowing I mean enough to you that you would hide this from me doesn't feel good. Why would I be upset when you've done so much to show me Eastlyn and more importantly you. I've been lied to so many times and by so many people that my gut reaction was anger. Miles, you didn't tell me one of the biggest things about you."

"I'm sorry, Mase."

"Thought you weren't going to apologize."

Fuck, I love this woman.

"I'm so glad you finally found me."

"Me too."

"What took you so long?"

CHAPTER 18

Mason

I've changed my clothes what has to be close to fifty times.

I've had my hair up, then down, and then back up again.

At the moment, it's down. I have on a casual red floral print dress that stops mid-thigh. I figure if I'm lucky on this beautiful Thursday, the length and flowy material will provide easy access for a certain CEO.

The day Miles revealed his real job, we talked at length about everything his role as president and CEO encompassed. He was clear that lots of travel came with the job, and he had only been around so much lately because it was harvest season.

I got my first taste of exactly what he meant that very same night. We had dinner with his parents later in the evening and then he dropped me off to go home and pack for his meeting with Luna Enterprises in San Francisco to discuss charitable and investment opportunities for EBC.

He's been gone for three days.

Three days since he told me how important I was to him.

Three days since thanking me for finally finding him.

Three days since leaving me sexually frustrated after *not* sleeping with me again!

If I thought I was hot and bothered for the man before our trip to the brewery, it was nothing compared to how I felt after talking for an hour in his office. What I wouldn't have given for him to rip my clothes off and take me on his leather couch. Hell, I would have been happy sprawled out on the dark wood of his desk after scattering its belongings all over the floor.

I just wanted him.

I thought for sure he would have come in with me after dinner with his parents, but instead, he told me to take the time he was away to really think about things. He said he wanted to be clear that he wasn't talking about anything temporary. He was all in, and he needed to know I was too.

He also said he was tired of me using the fact that I'll be going back to New York as a reason to say this was temporary. As far as he was concerned, it was a moot point, and we would deal with that when the time came.

Well, I've had time to think about it, and frankly, I'm sexually frustrated. I know my time in Eastlyn will be short-lived, but for the time being, I've decided to live in the moment. To see where things go and to make the time I *am* here count.

It's time to live in the here and now. If he can do it, then I can too.

Besides, I deserve a little happy.

Still trying to decide on what shoes to wear I'm balancing on one nude open-toed stiletto and checking the mirror to see if it's the one when there's a knock on the door.

"Eek!"

Squealing in frightened excitement, I kick my heel off and inadvertently hit the lamp on the bedside table.

Shit! He was supposed to text when he was headed this way.

Just knowing he's on the other side of my front door has my heart dropping to my stomach. I run out of the room, leaving the bedroom a disaster zone, bouncing off the furniture like a pinball on my way to answer his knock. When my thigh hits the corner of the sofa table in the living room, it hurts like a son of a bitch, and it's no doubt gonna leave a bruise, but there's no slowing me down.

I can't get to him fast enough, but when my fingertips touch the cool metal of the doorknob, I freeze. Taking in a deep breath, I needlessly smooth the front of my dress, trying to ease the nerves that are suddenly getting the best of me.

"I can hear you in there. Open the door, woman!"

I swing the door open to find Miles with suitcase in hand waiting for me impatiently.

"City Mouse, there you are. What took you so long?" He puts his bag in his other hand to push my hair behind my ear. "I missed you something awful."

"Is that so?"

"Came straight here from the airport."

He steps forward, forcing me to step back and let him in. He crosses the threshold and closes the door, placing his bag against the wall.

"I'm glad you did."

Standing in the middle of the room, we stare at each other, neither of us moving a muscle. My insides, however, are a nervous wreck and shaking something fierce.

Hands shoved in his pockets, sandy blond hair a mess from his clear rush to get here, T-shirt clinging to his broad shoulders, he is the epitome of sex on a stick. All confidence and bravado. Yet his eyes…his eyes are looking for something. Answers to something I'm not privy to somehow. I'm afraid if I speak first, I'll disappoint him by not giving him exactly what he's waiting to hear.

Thank God, he finally speaks.

"You have time to think about things?"

Oh shit. He was really serious about that.

Still afraid to speak I confirm I have thought about things with a nod.

"Cause, Mason, I'm about to make love to you all night long, but only if I know you're in. Like really in."

Whoa...did he say make love? As in love?

"I'm in."

"You sure?"

"I am."

"You gonna give it a rest when it comes to all this going back to New York talk?"

Animatedly, I zip my mouth shut and throw away the key.

"That's my girl. Get over here."

His arm wraps around my waist, pulling me tight against his hard torso. I'm pressed against an Adonis, but it's his words still bouncing around my head that have my heart melting and my core throbbing.

His lips land ever so lightly on my forehead, my cheeks, and finally my mouth. His tongue outlines my lips but doesn't seek refuge past them. He drugs me with his slow seduction, and my head is in the clouds.

"I missed you so much," I confess against his lips.

"Say it again." He sighs into my mouth, his breath filling me with life. In no rush at all.

"I missed you so much."

Holding my face oh, so gently, he pulls back to look at me.

Sincerity.

Genuine sincerity is what I see looking back at me.

"Mason O'Brien, what have you done to me?"

"Crackle?"

"I knew you felt it too."

"Miles…"

"Fuck it." He squats down so we're eye to eye. "I'm in love with you."

"What?" I ask, using the last breath left in my lungs to make sure I heard him correctly.

"I'm pretty sure I didn't stutter."

"You love me?"

"I do, and if you don't mind, I'd like to show you just how much."

"Miles…"

"Shh…no more talking."

He scoops me up in his arms, and this man who claims to have never been in love before carries me to the bedroom. When he sees the clothes thrown all around the room and all over the bed he had intended to place me on, he chuckles.

Setting me on my feet with care, I start to reach for the full wardrobe covering the bed, but he stops me.

"Couldn't decide what to wear, I see." With a smile on his lips, he kisses me on the cheek.

Without any other words, he tells me to stay put with his eyes. He casually cleans up my mess, placing things on the chair in the corner of the room. Before he's done, he makes a show of holding a pair of my lace panties up to his nose and taking a deep inhale.

The scrap of lace ends up in his shorts pocket instead of on the chair, and all my usual snappy comebacks are nowhere to be found. I'm having no trouble keeping quiet as he ordered in his oh, so sweet way.

Was he worried I wouldn't return his words of love and therefore he's playing it safe and cutting me off at the pass?

He turns his back, so he's facing the overflowing chair and lifts his shirt over his head, adding his contribution to the mountain of clothes. I only get a second to take in the perfection of his back before he turns toward me.

You could knock me down with a feather.

Yes, his chest is bare, and his abs are on display, but it's the lust in his eyes that has all reason leaving me.

His tan skin is bathed in the softness of the glow from the night's sky that is slowly slipping away, soon to leave us in the dark. For now, the white walls are painted with pink and orange hues of the setting summer sun sneaking in through the window.

I'm thinking he's going to lay me down on the now available bed. Instead, he walks up to me, slides his hand into my hair, and devours me with a kiss that has my breasts feeling heavy, my stomach tightening, and my legs quivering.

"I fucking need you, Mason." He breathes into my mouth, taking me in another all-encompassing kiss and not giving me the opportunity to reply.

He untangles one of his hands from my hair and traces my body as though he's memorizing my outline. His other hand now gently tickles down my neck, over my sternum, my breast, and when he gets just below my belly button, the anticipation is killing me. I know where I want his hand to go, and he does too. If only he wasn't slowly torturing me and prolonging his sweet seduction.

As I had hoped, my dress provides him easy access. He only has to inch it up ever so slightly, and with a little bend of his knees, one of his hands is caressing my ass.

I'm entranced by the electricity he's trailing all over my body while continuing to kiss me senseless. The feel of his fingertips remains where he touched me moments before even though his hand is now turning me so my back is to his front.

My dress continues to work as my ally when one of his hands slips under the front of my dress while his other is laid across my stomach, pressing me against his very large erection. My mind is just starting to register how an erection that size is going to fit when his finger slips under the lace not currently in his pocket.

His fingers work their magic while his lips burn a path up my neck so his tongue can trace the shell of my ear.

He must be able to feel my heart pumping with every scorching touch of my skin. How could he not? The thundering of my heartbeat fills my ears. The only other thing able to pierce its pounding is the sound of his breath sending me off into my own little world of ecstasy.

Bringing me to the edge of combustion, he removes his hand and releases my waist. Turning me around, he says, "Arms up."

Without hesitation, I do as requested, and my dress is over my head and on the floor. Taking a step back, he looks me over from head to toe but not in a demeaning way. He's admiring me. Lovingly.

Bringing his hand to his heart, he nearly brings me to my knees. "I have never seen anything so beautiful." He moves closer, erasing the space between us. "No sunrise or sunset could even come close."

"Miles…" I try to speak, but he interrupts me.

"Lie down, baby."

Without giving it a second thought, I once again do as he asks, and what comes next is a night bathed in moonlight and blanketed in bliss. He takes me to places I've never been and fills empty spaces I had no idea needed to be filled.

There are moments of softness and care while others are sheer unbridled passion and unadulterated pleasure.

We make love all night long and don't fall asleep until the early morning. All too soon, the sun's rays have made it to the bed. Pulling the sheet over my head, I refuse to open my eyes to the light of a new day. I'm not ready to face the realization that last night may have been a dream and I'd rather stay right where I am.

The dream beside me has no intention of avoiding the new day.

Joining me under the sheet, he kisses me gently before sliding down farther on the bed. He takes my nipple in his mouth and swirls his tongue around the now tight tip. His hands continue their exploring from a few hours earlier, and before I know it, without any words spoken, he slides down my body with his mouth guiding him to his destination and me to euphoria.

CHAPTER 19

Miles

"Smile!" Rachel holds up her camera, and we take the hundredth group selfie of the day. "I am gonna miss you guys so much," she says, turning to our little group. Reece wraps his arms around her but doesn't say a word. He doesn't need to. He has everything he needs right there pressed against his chest.

I've never seen the guy so happy. He has his girl back, and in a couple of days, they're leaving for Africa together. I've always been happy for my friends when they fall in love, but now, I look at my friend, and I feel it in a whole new way. Now, I understand how whole he feels to have her in his arms again.

There is no better feeling.

In fact, attending this wedding today and being surrounded by all of the love in the room have me even more certain than I was when I crawled out of her bed this morning of what exactly it is that I want in life.

Her.

Leaving her today was excruciating. After three nights and two full days living and breathing nothing but Mason, there were moments when I thought there was no way I would ever be able to leave.

Or walk again for that matter.

I was always pretty dang sure there was a heaven, but wondered what it might be like. Since Mason O'Brien walked into Eastlyn, I've been getting glimpses of it every time I see her face, but last night, she fortified my belief. I've been floating in heaven for the past couple of days, and all I want right now is to get back to it.

Don't get me wrong, today has been a blast. Drinking and dancing with my friends is always a good time. I just wish Mason was here with me.

When I told Scheana I would take her to the wedding, I thought for sure it was a promise I wouldn't have to keep because she and Adam would be back together, and they are. But he got a job out of town, and it includes working weekends, so here I am, at Brittany and Jason's wedding with Scheana instead of Mason.

Scheana's a fun girl, and we've had a great time, but the toasts have been made, cake has been cut, dancing has ensued, and I'm itching to get the hell out of here and back to my city mouse.

My city mouse who has hopefully had enough hours away from me to fill that journal of hers. I can picture her with her hair in a messy bun on top of her head, wearing her *Romance Writers Do It Better* oversized T-shirt and nothing else.

If our time locked away in Katie's house impacted her the way it did me, she can still feel me inside her and still smell me—not just on her sheets but everywhere. There hasn't been a moment of champagne and celebration when she hasn't been on my mind. Most prominent, though, is the space she's taking up in my heart.

I need to get out of here.

Back to Mason.

"Rach, you won't be gone forever, and we've still got tomorrow night. No goodbyes just yet," Amelia says, finishing the last sip of her bubbly.

"She's right," I confirm even though it will be a bummer to see her go. It always is when one of us leaves Eastlyn. "Tomorrow night, you can get sloppy drunk and tell us how much you love us, but right now, one of you needs to catch the bouquet."

Yes! A sure sign the festivities are coming to a close--the throwing of the bouquet.

The DJ asks all the unmarried ladies to gather, and they swarm like bees to honey.

"1…2…3!"

The flowers float through the air, and just as they should, they land in Rachel's hands. She blushes, the girls high-five her, and the guys pat Reece on the back.

"Now it's time for all those single men. Line up, gentlemen."

The first thing that crosses my mind is how good it feels not to be single. However, not many actually know this new bit of information. Since I'm not married, I find myself being dragged out to the middle of the dance floor where the girls just pushed and shoved each other for the bouquet.

We're given our own countdown, and when the silk elastic flies in our direction, my hand reaches up on instinct, and I snag it out of the air.

Like Reece, I'm met with pats to the back and hoots and hollers. Before Mason, I wouldn't have wanted the thing anywhere near me. Today, I shove the garter in my pocket, hoping it's a sign of things to come.

* * *

I HOPE it wasn't obvious that I was trying to drop Scheana off in a hurry. I know I'm an asshole, but I couldn't get her out of my truck fast enough. I tried my best not to be rude, but damn, did we have to recap the entire day on her front porch?

Fortunately, she lives only a few blocks from Katie's place, and I'm running up a new set of front steps in a matter of minutes. She's never seen me in a suit, so I'm looking forward to her reaction when she opens the door.

Knocking on the door and waiting for her to answer are a feat when all I want to do is barge through the damn thing so I can take her in my arms and tell her how much I missed her. Still not answering, I knock again, and when there isn't a reply, I'm about to do just that but relief washes over me when the door begins to open.

Thank God!

"Look what I got," I say, spinning the garter on my index finger. "Think it's a sign?"

My relief is quickly replaced by anxiety.

Her face.

The glow from this morning is a distant memory.

"What is it? What's happened, Mase?"

I step toward her only to be met with her palm on my chest, applying pressure to keep me back.

Away from her.

"What the hell is going on? Mason, talk to me."

"Nothing's going on. I'm just really tired and about to go to bed. Can we talk tomorrow?"

It's only nine. I know we didn't sleep much the past couple of days, but this is coming from the writer who stays up all night perfecting her craft. She's going to bed already? *I don't think so.*

"Mason, honey let me in."

She relents, pushing the door open. She walks away toward my bag next to the coffee table. "I went ahead and packed your things up for you so you're all set."

"You packed my things for me? I'm all set? What the hell happened while I was at that damn wedding?"

"Miles, I've just had time to think, and we both know how this is going to end."

"Do we now? Why don't you enlighten me?"

"Listen, I'll be gone in a few weeks, and there's no reason to get in any deeper when we both know it is just going to end. This way nobody gets hurt."

"Nobody gets hurt?" I don't mean to raise my voice, but what in the fuck is she talking about?

This already hurts!

Like a son of a bitch.

"Miles, please just go."

How does she not realize she's ripping my heart to shreds?

"I'm not going anywhere until you tell me what the hell I'm missing. What happened while I was gone?"

"I just can't do this again, okay?"

"Do what again?"

"This! You! I won't be that woman again. The woman who gets played. I won't do it, Miles!" she yells.

"How am I playing you, Mason? This is bullshit! You know that, right?"

"It's not. I saw the pictures the girls were posting today. I've lived this life before, and I can't do it again."

"What pictures?"

I have no idea what she's talking about. Did some old sex tape I'm not aware of somehow come to light?

She picks up her phone, taps the screen a couple of times, and then hands it to me. It's a picture of me and Scheana. We're on the dance floor, and she's bent over in front of me, and I'm pretending to spank her. It's funny.

"So?"

Ripping the phone out of my hand, she finds another picture and then shoves the phone back in my face. Okay, so in this one it looks like I'm licking her face. It was gross to her, and that was comical to me.

"What? Am I not allowed to have a good time?"

Still not replying, she takes the phone again, and this time, when she finds what she's looking for, she hits play and holds the phone up. A video of us on the dance floor plays. I'm in the center of the dance floor surrounded by my friends, I guess they do all happen to be women, and I'm doing what I do best. Being the life of the party. In the video, I dance my way around the circle of women and give them each a little twirl, some twerking for me and me acting like I like it. A couple of the older ladies get a kiss on the cheek, but it's really just me entertaining the wedding goers and myself while I'm at it.

"I still don't understand," I say genuinely.

"Miles, you're that guy."

"What guy is that?"

"The player. The one who needs all the attention, especially from women. The one who flirts. The one who kisses people on the cheek and dances suggestively with them. The kind of man who behaves like this!" she says, waving the phone an inch from my face. "The guy who inevitably does something he shouldn't when he has a girlfriend waiting at home for him."

"You're kidding, right?"

"Yes, you also dance with the grandmothers, and you're an equal opportunity flirt, but it's still not something I'm willing to put myself through again. I've been there. If I thought it hurt with Grant, I know it will hurt twice as much with you."

"I've told you this before but I guess you need to hear it again. I. Am. Not. Your. Ex."

"I know you aren't. But you are at the same time."

"Fuck that! You're scared and using this as an excuse because you know this is real!" I say, raising my voice.

"Don't yell at me!" she yells back.

"I'm sorry, but you've caught me off guard, and you're not making any sense," I say, trying to calm down but feeling frantic inside.

"Maybe not to you."

"Baby, my personality is one of the things you love about me. I know it is, and I also know you don't want to change me. You and I work the way we do without having to change each other. We fit, Mason."

Her eyes are glassy, one tear betraying her as it falls down her cheek.

"Baby, I love you. I don't see anyone else but you."

"You really think you love me?"

"I do. You're it for me."

"First loves never last."

"Tell that to Reece and Rachel."

Talking to the floor, she says, "You don't love me, Miles. I'm just the city girl who rolled into town for a few months. I'm different is all."

"Mason, please stop this." I lift her chin so she can't hide her eyes from me. Tears are streaming down her face. "I've never told another woman I love them, this is true, but it doesn't mean this won't last. Mase, you finally find me and make me fall in love with you, and now, you want to sit here and tell me my feelings aren't valid."

I wish today was like any other day when I could lighten the mood with a smart-ass comment, but I've got nothing. Instead, I seem to be having quite the opposite effect. More tears start falling from her beautiful eyes.

"Mason, baby. Don't cry. I love you. I am *in* love with you. Think what you want, but it's true."

"The thing is, I love you too, Miles. That's the problem. I can't love you because in the end you'll hurt me. In the end I live on the other side of the country."

"I knew it."

She fucking loves me.

Nothing has ever felt so good.

"What?" She sobs.

"You love me."

"But don't you see? It doesn't matter. It's too hard for me to be with someone like you. I can't put myself through it again. Besides, I'm leaving."

"But you can stay. You can write anywhere," I say, ignoring the part about me being too hard to be with.

"I can't," she says softly, stepping toward the front door. "I told myself I would never again give up my life for a man. I have to put myself first and moving to Eastlyn is not in the cards. I've worked too hard to get my life back. I refuse to lose it all again."

Her tears have dried. Her resolve has been found. She opens the door and closes her heart simultaneously.

"Mason, this is ridiculous. I would never ask you to give anything up." I plead with her, but she won't look at me. She's done with the conversation.

Done with me.

If she thinks this is it, she doesn't know me as well as I thought she did.

Grabbing my bag, I start to leave but stop in front of her where she stands with her hand on the doorknob, ready to shut me out the moment I cross the threshold.

"We aren't over, Mason, not by a long shot. I'll give you tonight, but I'm not giving up so easily. You're scared. I get it. But, baby, we're the real deal, and I fucking love you. Do you hear that?" Still looking at the ground, she gives me no reply. "And you fucking love me."

With my words lingering in the air, I leave.

Leave the house where I just experienced the best couple of days of my life.

The house containing the woman I love.

I'm not leaving for good, though.

She better believe I'll be back.

CHAPTER 20

Mason

"You guys, it's really sweet that you want to include me, but I don't think I'm up to going out."

"Nonsense! It's my last night in town for quite a while, and you already RSVP'd," Rachel says as she slides hangers back and forth in the closet.

I've gotten to know Rachel and Reece as well as the other ladies, and the way they've taken me in as one of their own in such a short span of time really is quite touching, but I still don't want to go out. Not when I know Miles is going to be there. Not even the adorable pixie cut blonde can make me feel like going out tonight.

"I RSVP'd when I thought I would be going with Miles. Tonight is for The Crew."

"And their significant others," Emmett chimes in from her spot on the bed.

"Well, I'm neither of those things."

She's lying down on the bed with her hands behind her head and her feet crossed. "Katie really has great taste. I wanna do a house swap with her when you're done. Oh, and you're funny, Mason. You really think you and Miles are over? Come on. We all know better."

"Listen, I've been here before. My ex was charming too. The life of the party. Everyone loved him, and his flirtatious nature was endearing. When in all actuality, it was just a way to cover up the fact he was sleeping with half the city. If he flirted with the little kids and the old ladies, then how could I get mad when he flirted with the young twentysomethings? He cheated on me for years, and no offense to you guys, but my friends all knew and didn't tell me. I'm not saying you would do the same, but these were friends I had had for most of my life. So, when I say I've been here before, I mean it. Sorry, Emmett."

"Mason, I am so sorry your ex was a lying, cheating bastard, but that just isn't Miles. He's fallen for you hard, and there's nothing he would do to jeopardize that. Miles lives life to the fullest, and he loves people, especially the people in this town. You can't ask him to stop living that way because you wouldn't have the feelings you have for him if you did."

Emmett's words are true. I wouldn't want him any other way.

"How do you know he's fallen for me?" I ask like an insecure teenager.

"Mason, listen." Amelia speaks up from the chair in the corner. "Miles Montgomery is loyal. Has he slept with a lot of women in this town and the surrounding counties? Sure. Has he ever really committed to any of those women? Nope."

"I know but..."

"He is committed to you, honey. I talked to him earlier, and he told me what happened. I told him I was sorry because it was all thanks to the pictures I posted while we were at the wedding, and you know what he said?"

"What?" I ask quietly but inside I'm screaming *WHAT?!*

"He told me not to sweat it. That he didn't do anything wrong, and he knows that you know that. He followed that up by saying he was in love with you, and he knew you loved him too and the two of you would figure it out. He said he didn't need to hide who he really was because you loved him, and you know deep down the man he is."

"He really said all that?"

"He sure did."

"Here, this is pretty," Rachel says, handing me the short little red sundress I had on when Miles got home on Wednesday night. "He told Reece the night we were all at The Jumps you were the one. Something about you finally finding him. So, why don't you get dressed and then we can all go so I'm not late to my own shindig."

Emmett sits up and pulls my hair tie out, fluffing my hair. "Yep, let's go so you can tell your guy you made a mistake and you're sorry for torturing him the past twenty hours or so."

"He's not my guy anymore. And I'm not wearing that."

"Oh, honey, if Miles says he's your guy, then he's your guy. Now put on the dress."

* * *

THIRTY MINUTES LATER, I'm in my red dress, but I've added a wide brown belt and a cropped jean jacket. We're sitting in the girls' favorite booth, and I've managed to tuck myself into the corner.

I'm trying my best to focus on the fun conversation about Emmett and I opening up a cute little new and used bookstore here in town that started while I was getting ready, but as amazing as the idea sounds and no matter how serious I may be about the topic, focusing on the details of the conversation is nearly impossible. Every time the door to the bar swings open, my gut wrenches in anticipation of him walking through it. When he doesn't walk through the door this time, I'm lost in my own head, wondering if he isn't here because of me. Have I hurt him so much he would miss tonight with his best friends?

Did he get in an accident on the way here?

Did something happen to Lou?

Where is he?

Why is he so late?

Why...

My thoughts are derailed by the breathtaking man who by simply walking through the door changes the atmosphere.

Crackle.

Finally.

I'm not changing my mind about being with him, but it doesn't mean I don't care.

That I don't love him.

Because dammit, I do.

But this time, I have to love myself more. I have to remember the pain and humiliation from before.

He knows where to find the girls and heads right to our table. He makes it no secret he sees me from across the bar. There never is any hiding from his eyes. Pulling my jean jacket closed in the front to hide the dress I have on underneath, I squirm in my seat, averting my eyes when he reaches the table.

"Ladies, what are we all drinking tonight? I've got the next round."

"Just EBCs for us and Beau's famous margarita on the rocks for Mason."

"No EBC for you tonight?"

"Not tonight."

I have a feeling my favorite beer would taste a tad bit bitter to me now. A reminder of what could have been.

"Wow, you really are stubborn," he says with new edge to his voice. His megawatt smile is turned down a notch or two. Yep, he's still pissed. "I'll bring a couple of pitchers of beer and one margarita over stat."

"I'm fine, thanks."

He ignores my comment but not me. There is a small smile on his face, but his eyes are full of sadness and somehow confidence all at once. As if to say, when are you going to pull your head out of your ass and stop hurting us both?

Oh, Miles, I wish I could. Trust me. It's better for us both to just end it now.

"Be right back."

"Daaaaamn, girl," Rachel says with dramatic flair. "I feel like I just watched a scene out of a movie. You've got him all spun up."

"I don't want to have him all spun up, Rachel," I whisper-yell across the table. I'm just trying to avoid the inevitable."

"You are insane, you know that, right?" Emmett questions me. "You're a writer. Why not just move here and write while he runs the company and the farm? You can travel with him, and you'd have a pretty plush life."

"I know I can write anywhere, but I've been the one to move before and look what it got me. Besides, I do just fine and live a pretty plush life all on my own. If I've learned one thing, it's that I don't need a man to take care of me."

I can hear the bite at the end of my statement, but I am so tired of being told *I can write anywhere.*

"No offense, sweetie. We just hate to see you go back to New York and most of all hate to not see things work out with the two of you. I didn't mean anything by it."

"I know you didn't, Emmett. Sorry, it's just a sensitive topic for me. Tonight is supposed to be all about Rachel and Reece anyway."

"Yes, it is," Reece says, taking Rachel's hand and pulling her up from the table and her seat next to me. "They're playing our song, babe. I'll have her back in about three minutes."

I'm watching them slow dance while Sam Hunt sings about cop cars when Rachel's abandoned seat to the left of me is filled with a presence I know all too well.

His big hands carried two pitchers of beer in one hand and a margarita in the other. He places the beer in the center of the table, then slides the margarita in front of me.

"In case you change your mind."

I can't help but think he means more than just my drink.

He knows he isn't playing fair by sitting next to me. Having him in my space like this is distracting, to say the least. We aren't touching, but we're close enough. The heat from his body is radiating off him, and his smell is infiltrating my senses. The Verdict suddenly feels stuffy, and without thinking, I slide my jacket off in the hopes I'll be able to catch my breath again.

"You have got to be shitting me?"

Crap. I forgot why I wore the jacket.

"What's wrong?" Amelia asks Miles from across the table.

"Oh, nothing, Melly. I was just reminded of something rather rudely, but I'm fine."

Emmett and Amelia stay silent on their side of the booth, and Amelia can't get out of the booth fast enough when Andrew arrives with his hand out dragging her away to dance.

"So, what's happening? What are you guys all chatting about?"

I want nothing more than to escape or at least run to the ladies' room for a second to collect myself, but that would mean asking him to move and having to slide past him, and I don't feel strong enough at the moment.

Oddly, I wasn't even strong enough to write in my journal after he left last night. I tried again today but just stared at the page. There has never been a time when I couldn't get what I was feeling on the page. Not wanting to put the truth down on paper. Because the truth of the matter is, I've fallen in love with a beautiful, kind man, and I've ruined it before it even had a chance.

The booth is beginning to close in around me.

My stomach is sick with anxiety.

Breathing seems nearly impossible.

"Excuse me," I say pushing on his arm. "I need to get out. Please move!"

"Mase, you okay?" There's concern in his voice, but I don't dare look into his eyes.

Clearly worried, he moves, letting me out of the booth.

Rushing to the bathroom, I can feel his eyes on me, burning my skin and taking away my ability to breathe. It isn't until I close the big wooden door and cut off his view to me that I can take my first breath since he sat down next to me. The cool water rushing over my wrists calms me, if only the glimpse of the woman staring back at me in the mirror above the sink didn't break my heart.

Not surprisingly, the door opens, and Emmett closes it behind her. Leaning against it, she looks at me with eyes full of pity.

"What was that all about?"

"Nothing. I think Beau's just a little heavy-handed with the tequila tonight. My margarita gave me a little scare. I'm good, though. Thanks for checking on me."

"You seemed fine until Miles sat down."

"Nah, it's all good."

"Mason, who are you trying to kid?"

"I don't know what you're talking about," I say, knowing she sees right through me. But for some reason, I feel the need to drag this out.

"Come on. You don't believe your own crap about not being able to be with him. It's obvious."

"Really?"

"Uh, yeah." Her face says I'm stupid for even asking.

"Do you think anyone else noticed?"

"Yes."

"Do you think Miles noticed?"

"Mason, he knows you better than the rest of us. Of course he noticed."

"Shit."

"He knows, and that's why he has no intention of giving up on you." She rubs my back sweetly. "Except you broke his heart."

"Emmett..."

"Why don't you go put it back together?" Her voice is sweet, yet underneath, I hear the sound of one of his chosen family members, a member of The Crew.

"Emmett, trust me. It's better to end it now."

"I don't want to hear the whole 'I'm going back to New York in a few weeks' crap."

She turns the faucet off, pulls two paper towels from the dispenser, and hands them to me. Clearly, my hiding out in the ladies' room has come to an end. The look on her face says she's not amused.

"Emmett, I think I'm gonna just go home," I say defeated.

"Oh no, you're not. I may not know you well, but I know enough to know you aren't a quitter. You, Mason O'Brien, are a strong, independent woman who is not going to let a night out get squashed because you can't stand to be in the same bar as Miles Montgomery."

"It's not like he did anything wrong, you know. He was just being himself after all. I'm just not sure if the strong woman I like to think I am is strong enough to be in a relationship with a man like him. As perfect as him?"

"Blech." She sticks her forefinger in her mouth like she's going to make herself throw up. "Whatever you do, never let him hear you call him perfect. We don't need things like that going to his overinflated head. We'll just keep that to ourselves. Sound good?" she says, pulling open the door.

I laugh, agreeing with her request.

The laughter is fleeting because as soon as we begin to cross the bar, our eyes lock, and as always, I find him watching me. Had he been watching the door, waiting for us to come back out? He's still sitting in the same spot he got up from for me, but when we get within a few feet, he gets up and walks away.

The booth now consists of Rachel, Amelia, Emmett, and myself. Miles and Reece are at the bar with a group of friends, but there is a rope of tension between us pulled so tight if one of us loosens our grip, we'll go tumbling to the ground.

I sip my margarita while the girls tell stories about growing up in Eastlyn, and even though I hear every word and laugh at the appropriate moments, my mind is never off the CEO farm boy at the bar.

Thirty minutes later, out of the corner of my eye I see Miles dragging a middle-aged woman onto the dance floor. He spins her in and out and all around the hardwoods.

"Rach, looks like your parents are here, but as per usual, Miles stole your mom already," Amelia points out.

"Of course, he did. She thinks that boy hung the moon. She needs his kind of fun tonight, though. She's so stressed about me going to Africa." She's looking at me when she speaks. Telling me without words that this is what he does. He makes people feel good.

From the looks of it, Rachel isn't kidding. Her mom is all smiles, and you can hear her squeals of delight all the way over here.

There's no keeping my eyes off him or the smile from my face.

He's right.

This is one of the reasons I love him.

He's a flirt.

But in the best way.

He makes people happy.

He dances with them.

He jokes with them.

He makes them feel good.

He makes *me* feel good.

The song changes, and Rachel yells, "Let's go girls!"

Emmett pulls me out of the booth, dragging me behind her to the dance floor where everyone is lining up in rows.

Shit. It's a line dance. The only line dance I know is the electric slide, and this isn't it.

"Emmett!" I yell over the music, trying to pull away from her. "I don't know this dance!"

"Come on. Just follow along, and you'll pick it up quick."

"No, really. I'm just gonna…"

His big hands grab my hips. His breath floats over my hair when he says, "I'll teach you."

I don't resist. And I don't tell him no.

Instead, I do the opposite and let him guide me through the dance. I trip over my own feet, I bonk my head with his a couple of times, and I laugh. Just like Rachel's mom.

Why?

Because that's what Miles does.

I know he's not Grant, and I also know I've never laughed like this with him. But as soon as the song ends, the insecurity comes flooding back, and I try to make a fast break. Grabbing my hand, Miles has other ideas. Much to his joy and my dismay, the next song is a slow one.

Pulling me into his arms like we're at a high school dance, we sway back and forth while the other couples on the dance floor two-step around us. We don't speak and to avoid eye contact I press my forehead against his shoulder.

Internally, I know it looks like I'm caving already, but like Emmett said, I'm not a quitter. I've made a decision, and I'm going to stick to it. I won't cause a scene, though. I'm going to finish this dance, then go home.

When the song ends, I finally brave a look up, and where I thought I would find his usual charming smile I'm met with a face serious as a heart attack.

My stomach starts to feel queasy again.

"Thanks for the dance. I'm gonna head home."

"You walk?"

"I'll be fine. It's still light out."

"I'll walk you."

Walking away from him, I yell over my shoulder and the Thomas Rhett song now playing. "No thank you. I'll be fine."

He yells back, "Meet you by the door after you've said your goodbyes."

Great.

The group is standing near the bar, watching us. Miles gets to them before me. I do my best to ignore him and focus on the girls as I tell them goodbye.

"Rachel, it was great to meet you, and I hope your trip is amazing. I really appreciate you including me tonight, but I'm gonna head home."

"Thank you for coming. I know you weren't really in the mood." She smiles, pulling me into a hug. "Give him a shot. I think you'll be surprised to find he won't let you down." She gives me a squeeze, and when she pulls back, she gives me a wink and motions toward the door with her head. "Someone's waiting for you."

Sure enough, Miles is at the exit leaning against the wall.

Not sure what else to say to her, I wish her and Reece safe travels waving at the rest of the group and apprehensively cross the bar. Before I reach him, he pushes the door open with one arm and wordlessly ushers me through with his free hand.

There aren't any words exchanged on the walk home, but the way he takes my hand, linking my fingers with his and not letting go until we reach the front door clearly says he's not giving up. He stands with his hands in his pockets with no intention of moving.

"It was really nice of you to walk me home," I say, staring intently on the keyhole while I unlock the door. Anything not to look at the eyes I avoided all the way here. "I'm sure they're waiting for you, though, so good night and thanks again."

"Why did you wear that dress tonight?"

Shit.

"Why, what's wrong with this dress?"

I'm playing stupid, but I don't know what else to say or do.

"Mase, give me a break."

"Listen, thanks again. Have a good…"

He cuts me off. "Let's just stop with all of the bullshit, shall we?"

"What bullshit? I'm just saying good night."

"Why did you wear the dress you were wearing the first time I made love to you?"

I stare at my feet, feeling what I don't know.

"Were you trying to hurt me even more than you already had?"

"I didn't think you'd notice."

"I notice everything about you, Mason."

"I'm sorry, I wasn't thinking. I wasn't even gonna go, but the girls showed up and dug through my closet, and this is what they threw at me to put on."

"You had no control over what you wore tonight? You're trying to blame the girls for wearing something you knew would have an impact?"

"I guess I didn't give it much thought."

"You did too, and you know what?"

"What?"

"I'm glad you wore it because it means you care. You wanted a reaction, and you sure as shit got one."

I'm not big on lying, lying to myself excluded, so I don't reply to his assumption.

"Well, have a good rest of your night. I'll see you around," I say to the stubborn man infiltrating my space.

Be strong, Mason.

Do not ask him to come in.

"I'm not going anywhere, Mason."

He's serious. He doesn't sound angry, but he does sound deadly serious.

"Come on, it's Reece and Rachel's going away. Everyone is expecting you to come back."

"I'm taking them to the airport in the morning. It's all good."

"Miles…"

"If you don't mind me coming in, I'd like to talk."

He's keeping his hands to himself, but the softness in his eyes pierces through me, grabbing me with all his might and not letting go.

I turn away from him and walk inside, leaving the door open behind me. He follows, closing the door and locking it once he's in the house. I slip my shoes off and strategically collapse in the overstuffed armchair only meant for one. If I'm going to keep my wits about me, I cannot give him the opportunity to get too close.

Instead of taking a seat, he picks up one of the fifty throw pillows on the couch and paces the room with it pulled tight to his chest.

"Mason, I want you to know that I hear you."

Making sure I'm listening, he stops to look at me, really look at me, while still hugging his pillow.

"I know you've been hurt before, and I know because of this you have your guard up, but your whole plan to end things now before they've really started isn't going to work for me."

Now the pillow is behind his head. And I can't help but stare at his toned biceps. It's completely inappropriate to be checking him out right now, but I am only human, after all. And they're huge!

"You see, I'm not your ex. I'm not going to hurt you. How could I when I've been waiting for you for so damn long?"

He and his pillow finally drop to the couch. He sits on the edge, getting as close to me as he can. Our knees are a breath apart, but he doesn't try to touch me.

"If I'm being honest, it hurts when you compare me to him. I don't deserve it. I'm nothing like him, and I'd really like the chance to prove it to you."

My heart betrays me, my head and my body following suit when I reach for his hand.

"Mason, I know your life is in New York, and I know it makes our situation seem impossible to you, but why don't we give us a chance before you go throwing hurdles in the way? I'm a man of means, and you can write anywhere. I'm not asking you to move your life, but I am asking you to see the possibility of us."

Standing in front of me, he offers me his hand.

"City Mouse, I'm exhausted. These past twenty-four hours were harder on me than an entire harvest. I don't care if we keep our clothes on and sleep on top of the covers, but I'm sleeping with you in my arms."

"Miles, I..."

"Just stop, Mason."

I don't know if it's my own exhaustion or knowing that he's right.

Heck, everyone is right.

I'm crazy about him, and the only thing I want to do is to crawl into bed with him and sleep in his arms.

So I take his hand, and we walk silently to the bedroom.

Waiting to see if I want to sleep on top of or under the covers, he crosses his arms over his chest, letting me take the lead.

Pulling back the bedding, I slip off my dress and climb into bed. He strips down to nothing but his underwear and crawls in with me. He lies on his back, holding his arm open to me, and I rest my head on his shoulder.

My arms wrap around him, and my leg is tangled between his. He kisses me on the top of the head, and we hold each other.

He doesn't try to keep explaining why he's different or how we'll deal with the distance. He simply holds me close while simultaneously giving me the space to think.

The possibility of us.

CHAPTER 21

Miles

The pale light of the morning illuminates the softness of her face while my sweet city mouse sleeps. We're both lying on our sides mirroring one another, the only difference between us is her peaceful slumber. In stark contrast, I am wide-awake with my insides twisted in knots.

Even if I do have all the confidence in the world that the woman lying next to me is the one I've been waiting for, I also know life doesn't always work out the way we hope. We don't always get what we want.

The thing is, lying here, watching her sleep, yes, I want her, but more than that, I *need* her. In a few short weeks, I've discovered the missing piece of me, and there is no more me without her.

I need her to breathe.

But she's made it very clear the need does not go both ways. After what she's been through, she's learned to compartmentalize and only need what she can provide for herself. As much as I want her to need me as much as I need her, the strength she's found in herself is one of the things I love about her, and I wouldn't want to change her.

But I do *want* her to need me.

She's been burned by those closest to her, and the only person who has ever put Mason first is Mason.

What she doesn't get quite yet is that she's not alone anymore. She has me. And I will always put her first. Her best interests and her happiness will always be my priority.

Her slightly parted lips are begging to be kissed, her sun-kissed shoulders are pleading with me to touch them. But I don't.

I'm frightened to wake her. Afraid to hear what she might say. I know she was awake for quite some time last night because I never did sleep, aware of every breath she took. I felt it when she did finally fall asleep. Her breath grew heavy, and her body almost imperceptibly grew more lax.

With her asleep in my arms, everything was as it should be. Eventually, she grew warm and rolled away, but not long after, she rolled back over to face me and reached for me in her unconscious state.

Did she finally fall asleep because she had thought about us, like I asked her to, and she had come to a conclusion? Or was she so exhausted from it all that her body took over for her brain and let her sleep?

As much as I want to wake her, it's way too early, but I have to take Reece and Rachel to the airport, and Lou needs to be fed and let out before I pick them up. Reluctantly, I slide out of bed, gather my clothes, and creep into the living room to get dressed.

Looking for a piece of paper and a pen, so I can leave her a note, I stumble upon one of her infamous journals, and it calls to me like a beacon in the dawn. I pick it up but stop myself before I do something I'll regret. Reading her journal would break her trust on a level I'm not sure she would get over, but I sure as hell want to. I've been dying to know what she's written about her time in Eastlyn, but most importantly what she's written about me.

I put the multicolored book down and instead flip over the Eastlyn Rodeo Days flyer sitting on the kitchen table and write my note on the back. I prop it up against the vase of flowers in the center of the table and let myself out. It doesn't go unnoticed by me that the flowers look like one of the window displays from Busy Bee Flowers. She said she'd be back for flowers, and she did just that.

Hell yes, she did.

Another reason to fight with all my might for her.

For us.

* * *

Halfway to the airport, Reece and Rachel start asking questions. Frankly, I'm shocked it took this long.

"So, Mason, huh?" Reece asks without really asking anything, but of course I know what he's asking.

"What about her?"

"Stop it, Miles. How did it go last night? You didn't come back to The Verdict, so is that a good sign that you made her see she was making a huge mistake?"

"That right there is the million-dollar question, Rachel. We talked, and we slept, but nothing was resolved."

"Man, I'm sorry to hear it. She's a good girl." Reece commiserates with me.

"You don't even know the half of it, man. I've finally found the woman I want to commit to, and she doesn't need me. Lives on the other side of the country and won't stop reminding me how limited her time here in Eastlyn is."

"Miles, you know the girls and I have talked, and you have to know it's not about you, right? She's been through some stuff.

Been screwed over and lost herself there for a time, so she's scared."

I love that she confided in the girls when she doesn't trust other people easily. Rachel taking her side means my crew has accepted her.

"I know, Rach, and I'm not trying to rush her into something, but it's really hard when it seems so easy for her to just walk away from me when she gets scared. I know I'm new to this whole relationship gig, but I've learned a lot from all of you, especially you two. I know communication is key, and she has to talk to me."

"Be patient. I know it's hard but trust me. I know a little something about the right girl being worth the wait." Reece turns in his seat to look at Rachel.

In the rearview mirror, I watch her mouth, "I love you too, Reece." Now, these two have really been through it.

"Enough about me! Look at you two! I couldn't be happier for you guys. Rach, you excited?"

"I can't freaking wait, but I'd be lying if I said I wasn't scared to death."

Now Reece is completely turned in his seat. "What do you mean you're scared to death? I'll be with you the entire time."

Uh-oh.

"Babe, I know you will be, but I also know you run that place. You're gonna be busy, and not only am I gonna be the new girl in town but these people are also your friends and co-workers. I don't know. I can't help but be nervous."

Reece works with Doctors Without Borders and runs a refugee camp for thousands of people who have nothing and need assistance. She's right. He is busy. Busy saving lives.

"Rachel, you know you are going to be breaking some hearts when you come back with him, right? I'm sure our hot, young doctor here has all the other volunteers creaming in their panties, and now you've taken him off the market. You better watch your back, girl."

"Come on, Vi," Reece says, using his longtime nickname for her. She was so quiet and shy as a kid that he called her Violet, as in shrinking violet. "Ignore Miles. He doesn't know what he's talking about."

"You better hope he's wrong because the days of me being shy and quiet are long gone. I don't want to have to cut a bitch, but I will if push comes to shove."

"Hot damn! That's my girl!" I hoot from the driver's seat.

Reece, well, he isn't sure what to say. He's just staring at her stunned silent.

"Understood, babe?" she asks the love of her life, who's seeing a part of her he's missed over these past twelve years.

The one positive thing Rachel gained after her heart was torn to shreds was her voice. She protected herself and her heart after Reece ended things with her, and she has been fierce ever since.

I see similarities between her and Mason. Here's to hoping Mason has found her voice yet is still willing to give us a chance. If Rach can give Reece a second chance, I sure as hell hope Mason can give me a first.

"Understood, *babe*. God, I love you."

"We're here, lovebirds," I say, putting the truck in park at the curbside drop-off at our small regional airport in Pendleton. They'll take a quick flight to Portland where they'll grab their international flight.

We all hop out, and I help them unload their luggage. I'm grateful I got the privilege of driving them today, even if it meant leaving my sleeping beauty. I'm glad to have had a bit of one-on-one time I wasn't able to get last night at their going-away festivities.

"Thanks for the ride, Miles." Rachel gives me a hug and whispers in my ear. "Be patient with her, Miles. If Reece and I can make it work again, you guys will get there too."

"Thanks, Rach. I sure hope you're right." I pull back from her and hold her at arm's length to get a good look at her. "Be safe and enjoy this time. I know it isn't going to be all fun and games, and it will be hard to be romantic but enjoy this experience with him, okay."

She nods.

"Love you, girl."

"Right back atcha."

Rachel steps aside, and Reece steps in to fill her place.

"Thanks for the ride, man. When I get back in six months, I hope that sweet girl is by your side."

"Thanks, Doc. Now get out of here and go save the world."

The good doctor and his shrinking violet smile, wave, and head off on their adventure.

CHAPTER 22

Mason

When I woke up this morning, I was disappointed not to find his beautiful blond head on the pillow next to me, but after reading the note he left for me in the kitchen, I'm relieved to have had the morning to myself.

Miles pulls no punches when it comes to finding his way into my heart, and his words have really hit home. I must have read his note twenty times, committing his writing and his words to memory.

City Mouse,

Please don't stumble over something that's already behind you.

Remember, I am not your past, but I would love to be your future or at the very least your present. I know I already said it last night, but just remember, I'm not asking you to move your life, I'm simply asking you to think about the possibility of us.

Have a good day,

CHAPTER 23

P.S. Let's talk over dinner. Pick you up at 6:00.

Now, here I am, getting ready for my dinner date after a day spent doing what I do when I have a lot on my mind.

I nested.

I did laundry. I swept the floors. I cleaned the bathroom. Organized.

I may not be pregnant, but this is what I do when my brain won't stop and it's not because of a story I need to get down on the page. It's what I do to find a way to control a situation out of my control. Even though this situation appears to be completely in my control, I have no control over my feelings for Miles.

And. That. Scares. Me.

Hence, the nesting.

As organized as everything is, I shouldn't be standing here staring into the closet like I have no clue what's inside, but here I am. I didn't pack for dinner dates or to impress a man. I packed for hot summer days and long, late nights at my computer. Of course dinner could be at The Jury Room, or it could be at Tom's for milkshakes.

Either way, tonight feels important.

Have I made any decisions? I'm not sure I have.

He did ask me to consider the possibility of us and not whether or not I was moving here or marrying him. Just considering the possibility of what could be. When I think of it that way, my nerves settle enough for me to pull a dress off its hanger and get ready.

It's hot as Hades outside, but I leave my hair down, taking my time to add big curls that I tamed into long, loose waves. My peach floral dress hits me mid-thigh—like I know he likes —and with my three-inch wedges on, my legs look ten feet long.

Too much for a weekday dinner?

Not enough for a night with Miles?

My time to deliberate is over with the sound of a knock on the front door.

Suddenly, the air-conditioned house is crazy hot, and I'd give anything to have my hair up off my neck. My heart beats like the wings of a hummingbird, and the nerves that are stirring up in my stomach are irrational. Just knowing he's here has me hot and bothered, shy and nervous.

Rushing to the door, I tell myself, *it's only Miles*. The man you've felt so comfortable around these past weeks. He's your friend. A good man. He cares about you.

Just. Calm. Down.

My hand, clammy palm and all, turns the doorknob, and the instant my eyes take him in, I know my worries have been illfounded.

I love this man.

Every larger than life, CEO, flirty, farm boy piece of him.

As he stands in front of me sans hat but wearing a small smile and a sparkle in his caramel eyes, there is no doubt in my heart, mind, body, and soul how I feel about him.

He's been at the office today if the polo and dark jeans are any indication. I much prefer his version of CEO over the stuffed shirt version, but I prefer his farm boy jeans and T-shirt look even more.

"Baby, I know it's Monday, but damn if you don't look like a Saturday night."

"Thank you."

"You gonna let me in, or you just gonna stand here letting all the cool air out?"

Stepping aside, I let him in and shut the door behind us.

He only takes a couple of steps away from the door before turning to face me. Staring into my eyes, he searches my soul for the meaning of life.

Pressing my back against the front door and closing it in the process, I try to find the words to properly tell him how I feel. If only I could say all the right things like my characters do in my books. If ever there was a time when I wouldn't mind life imitating art, this would be it, but no such luck.

"I got your note."

"Yeah?" He takes a step closer, placing himself a few small breathless inches between us.

"Yeah."

"And?" His boots shuffle closer, and his one-word question flutters across my skin.

There's no controlling myself when my lips press against his, and he opens up for me. He grips my hip, and with his chest pressed against mine, I'm melting into the door as our bodies try desperately to become one.

The muscles of his back flex under my fingers while he flexes something else against my belly.

"So, does this mean you're giving us a chance?" he asks against my lips.

"What do you think?"

He stops the kissing and heavy petting, pressing his forehead against mine.

"I think you love me, and you're scared."

"I think you're right."

"But still, you love me."

"I do."

He kisses me on the nose.

"And I love you. I'd say that's a pretty good place to start."

"It is."

He pulls back just enough to look me in the eyes.

"You love me just the way I am, City Mouse?"

Is that a blip of insecurity hanging off Miles Montgomery, or is he just making sure I know he is what he is and he's not changing. Either way, I do love him just the way he is.

"I do."

"Say it."

"Say what?" I tease, knowing full well what he wants.

"Give me the three little words I need to hear."

"What words would those be?"

His big calloused hand cradles my face as his thumb caresses my cheek. His eyes beg me to say the words. And there's no possible way to deny him.

"I love you, Miles. All of you."

Expecting his charming smile after getting his way, I'm surprised by the serious look on his face.

His thumb continues to brush over my cheek and his eyes no longer searching mine speak directly to me. They thank me for loving him. For giving him a chance. For giving us a chance.

"I love you too, Mason." He places a sweet kiss on my lips, and I melt on the spot. "Come on, if we don't leave now, we'll never make it to dinner."

"That's fine with me."

After separating himself from me, he adjusts the bulge in his pants. When I step toward him, he steps away from me, knowing my dastardly plan to keep us in all night.

"Don't you worry, baby. You'll get what you're looking for, but first, I need to feed you. Why don't you throw some things in a bag? We're staying at my place tonight."

"Oh, we are, are we?"

"If you don't mind, Lou would sure appreciate it."

"Oh, well if it's for Lou, then of course."

Quickly, I throw some things in an overnight bag while floating around the house like I've been sprinkled with pixie dust and wondering how I could have ever had my doubts.

CHAPTER 24

Mason

The past two weeks have been blissful.

No matter how busy he may be running his company and checking on the farm, I see Miles every day and spend every night in his arms.

Neither of us has brought up New York or how many weeks I have left.

It's six and a half, but who's counting.

We're living in the here and now, and it's pretty great.

I've never laughed this much.

I've never orgasmed this much.

I've never felt so cherished.

Today is the first time I've felt a twinge of insecurity since I've decided to give us a chance.

The anticipation of meeting his grandparents for the first time, at Sunday dinner no less, has me a little jittery. He asked me to come last Sunday, but I was in the zone and had to keep writing. Book one in my new series is almost done, and I do believe I may actually have it to my editor well before my deadline.

They say there's a first time for everything.

I've had dinner with his parents several times now, and I really like them. But meeting Pops and Granny feels like I'm about to take a final exam or something.

What happens if I fail this test? His family is everything to him.

"What's going on in that wicked smart head of yours?" Miles asks from the driver's seat.

"Honestly?"

"Nah, lie to me and tell me you were having a wild sex fantasy about me."

I slap away his hand now playfully making its way up my thigh. "Stop it, you heathen."

He takes my hand in his and kisses the back of it. "I may be a heathen, but I'm your heathen."

"Yes, you are. But will you still be mine if your grandparents don't approve? I know how important they are to you."

"Is that what's had you in your head all day?"

I shrug.

"Babe, they're going to love you! You have nothing to worry about."

"You don't know that."

"Oh, but I do. Everyone who meets you falls head over boots for you, there's not a thing about you not to love."

"Head over boots, huh?"

"Did I stutter?"

"Seriously, though. What if?"

"Mason, you really need to stop worrying. Mom and Dad love you. The Crew love you. Hell, Mel the barber loves you. You're really worrying over nothing."

"I sure hope you're right."

"Besides, all they care about is whether I'm happy. And Mason...you make me very fucking happy."

"Right back atcha, cowboy."

"See, there's nothing to worry about."

By the time I hear the crunch of rocks under the truck's tires, his reassurances have settled me a bit, and I've found a sliver of my confidence as we begin our drive down a tree-lined gravel road. Trees so tall they had to have been here for decades shelter us from the hot sun leaving fantastical shadows all around us. Beyond the massive trees lining the small road are acres of endless green grass with more giant trees perfectly placed here and there, providing shadows of shade and adding to the beauty of the landscape. And at the end of the road sits the most perfect house.

The house is grand but not massive. A white two-story country house with black shutters, a dream-worthy wraparound porch, and the dark blue of a lake as its backdrop.

Breathtaking.

Magical.

"Miles, it's beautiful. Are you sure we haven't just driven right into a Nicholas Sparks novel?"

"Isn't that *The Notebook* guy?"

"Yes, and about a hundred other novels set in romantic places just like this. How was this not on the tour?"

"Well, I took you to meet my parents, and that was pretty ballsy for so early on, don't ya think?"

"You could say that." I laugh.

"I figured that was enough to start with. Didn't want to scare you away." He gives me an endearing grin in place of his usual megawatt smile. "Besides, this is a first for me, so I needed to be sure you were in."

"A first?"

"City Mouse, the firsts with you are endless. I've never brought a girl to meet Pops and Granny because I always knew with them there was no need if I wasn't bringing home the real deal."

"The real deal, huh?"

"Yes, ma'am. Besides, I have a sneaking suspicion you're going to like Elsie Lake."

"Elsie Lake? That must be the lake behind the house?"

"Well, that's what Pops named the part of Eastlyn lake that the house sits on. Named it after Granny Elsie."

"Aw, he named a lake after her. How sweet is that?"

"Well, she's the love of his life, Mase. My grandparents have been together since they were teenagers, and they're still as much in love with each other today as they were back then. Like I told you before, I've grown up with some pretty great examples of what people in love look like."

"Wow, we really are entering the land of *The Notebook*, aren't we?"

After he puts the truck in park, his chest rises with a deep breath. He inhales and his chest falls when he lets it out. Clearly, I'm not the only one who's nervous.

"It'll be fine, remember?"

Shaking off the emotions he thought he was keeping hidden beneath the surface, he smiles and kisses the back of my hand again.

Today means a lot to him.

It means a lot to me.

Another page in our book is turning.

Holding hands, we take the steps up to the screen door together. When we walk over the threshold, his Eastlyn Beer Company hat comes off his head and is placed on a coat rack next to the front door. He runs his hands through his hair before kissing me on the cheek and pulling me down the hall behind him.

The hallway walls are covered in black and white family

photos and a sweet floral wallpaper. Wallpaper isn't my thing, but this works.

When we enter the kitchen, I'm knocked senseless by the delicious smells filling the air. The strongest scent is that of a freshly baked apple pie. I can't remember the last time I've been in a kitchen with an actual apple pie baking in the oven.

Heaven.

Miles's mom, Krista, is washing her hands over a white farmhouse sink, and a smaller woman with a short silver bob works over the most beautiful chef's stove. The house may be a century old, but the kitchen has clearly been updated. All black and white tiles with stainless top-of-the-line appliances. However, as it should be, the décor still has that country feel. Amongst the high tech finery are roosters, cows, and adorable pigs perfectly placed.

The nerves come rushing back at the sight of the tiny woman, and Miles squeezes my hand back when my grip on his tightens. He wastes no time making our presence known in an oh, so Miles fashion.

"And how are two of the most beautiful women on the planet?"

"Oh, my sweet boy is here!" His grandmother's eyes sparkle like her grandson's often do, and with her hands in the air, she steps away from her burners. "Get over here and give your granny some sugar!"

He releases my hand and embraces his grandmother while Krista dries her hands with a towel before pulling me into a welcoming hug. She releases me but stands next to me, shoulder to shoulder, arms crossed.

Is something wrong?

"So now, we're two of the most beautiful women on the planet when we used to be *the* two most beautiful women on the planet." Her elbow nudges my arm.

With his arm wrapped around the adorable matriarch of the

family, they turn with matching sparkle shooting at us from across the room.

"Ah, Mom. You're both still in my top three. But I mean, look at her. She's pretty amazing, don't you agree?"

Before Krista can reply, Elsie exclaims, "Oh, Miles, I couldn't agree more. You must be Mason. Here, stir this," she says, handing Miles the large spoon in her hand.

He does as he's told, and she crosses the beautiful dark wood floors with her arms wide open once again.

"It's so nice to meet you, my dear." She pulls me down to hug her, treating me like I'm already part of the family. "I've heard so much about you from not only my grandson but from Mitch and Krista too, and I'm so happy to finally meet the girl who has my sweet boy's heart wrapped around her little finger."

Whoa.

"It's very nice to meet you too, Mrs. Montgomery."

"Call me Granny, and if you're not ready for that, call me Elsie. But only for now." She winks and directs me to one of the stools at the kitchen island. "Sit, and tell me all about yourself."

"Oh no, I don't want to just sit here while all of you cook."

"Don't worry, from here on out, we'll keep you busy helping, but today, you tell me all about yourself." She takes the spoon from Miles and places herself back at the stove. "You, go on and get. Your dad and Pops are out back. Go say hello and give us ladies some time to ourselves. Go on and get."

"Yes, ma'am."

Miles breezes out of the kitchen but not without closing the blinds on the window above the kitchen sink, placing a kiss on my cheek, and leaving me with a whisper of, "*I love you*," in my ear.

* * *

THIRTY MINUTES LATER, my life story has been told.

My reward, childhood stories about Miles. Sweet stories, hilarious stories, and stories revealing what makes him the man he is and have me falling deeper in love with him than I was when we pulled up the gravel drive.

Behind me, the bang of a slamming door signals the men. Most importantly, Pops, who I haven't met yet.

"Well, well, well. If it isn't the famous writer."

I'm off my stool in a flash and turning around to greet Miles, Mitch, and the man who began Montgomery Farms decades ago. It feels like I'm meeting the president or something.

"Mr. Montgomery, it's nice to meet you."

My extended hand is trembling, but it doesn't matter because he doesn't take it.

"Sorry, my dear. We're huggers in this family," he says, wrapping his big arms around me. He asks me to call him Pops or George. His father was Mr. Montgomery.

"Thank you, for having me, George. You have a beautiful home."

"And you're quite the beauty as well. I see what has my grandson so smitten. Brains and beauty are hard to come by. Isn't he a lucky boy?"

I guess the Montgomery genes are pretty strong. It's pretty clear where Miles gets it.

We chat for a couple of minutes before Miles asks his grandmother how long we have until dinner. She tells him he has twenty minutes before he has to set the table and he says we'll be back in time to do just that.

He takes my hand, and we walk out of the kitchen and out the French doors that lead outside.

"Miles, they're great. Thank you so much for bringing me along today."

"You're welcome…"

"Oh, and your Granny loves you so much and…"

"Mason."

"…Miles, she is so proud of you, and you look so much like Pops and your dad of course, but…"

"Mason, baby."

"Sorry, am I rambling?"

"You are."

"Sorry, but they're just so…"

He kisses me to shut me up. His method is effective, and I'm no longer thinking about his grandparents.

"Mason?" he says against my lips.

"Miles?"

"Will you please look to your right?"

"Okay…"

I interrupt myself this time with an audible gasp.

Turning my body away from him and toward Elsie Lake, I never could have expected this.

A lake with a long dock taking you over the water and ending with two white Adirondack chairs.

It's the EBC logo.

In front of me is a living, breathing Eastlyn Brewing Company logo that I've taken a hundred pictures of.

Only the reality is so much better than the label.

The breeze is blowing the weeping limbs of the trees hanging over the lake. The water ripples from the graceful landing of a goose. The sound of frogs echo in my ears, and a golden retriever is basking in the sun in the grass in front of us.

It's beautiful.

Without a word, he takes my hand, and we walk through the grass until we reach the dock where he stops us.

"You said one day you wanted to sit here and drink a beer with someone special. I have the beer, and if I'll do for that someone special, what do you say we have that beer?"

"Miles, I don't even know what to say."

For some reason, my eyes fill with tears, but I only let one escape. Am I crying over a beer logo come to life?

"Come on," he says, not calling attention to the tear.

Walking on the wood planks with my hand in his is surreal, to say the least. When we reach the two white wooden chairs, he says, "Take your pick."

I take the one on the right because that's the one I always imagined sitting in, but I don't sit down. He pulls two bottles of EBC out of his shorts pockets along with a bottle opener.

He pops the top of each bottle, puts the caps in his pocket, and hands me my beer, lifting his up in the air.

"Cheers to dreams coming true, baby."

I tap the neck of my bottle with his. "Cheers to dreams coming true."

We each take a sip, and then I turn and just stare at the chairs.

"Go ahead, it won't bite," he says, giving my shoulder a little nudge with his.

"You sure?"

"Uh, that's what they're here for. Sit, woman."

Doing as instructed, I sit in the chair on the right, and when my butt has finally hit the seat, he takes the chair on the left.

We sit there in silence with the sound of the wind rustling the leaves and that same breeze caressing our skin, reminding us to live in the beauty of the moment.

To be present.

To see the gifts we've been given.

Twenty minutes have gone by and Miles leaves to set the table and to give me a few minutes on my own.

It's still light out, but it's that time of the evening when the mosquitoes have arrived. When they land on the water, the circles they leave on the surface mesmerize me, but I know all too well how those same mosquitoes love the way I taste, and I know it's best if I get inside before they begin feasting on me.

Getting up from my chair and leaving the dock is the hardest thing I've done today. But if I'm lucky, I'll be back.

* * *

Dinner is great and the fresh baked apple pie for dessert even better. The conversation is light and constant, consisting of everything from the success of harvest to Rachel and Reece in Africa and Stacci's impending due date.

Something is mentioned about Miles and New York, but Krista shushes Mitch and tells them there will be no business at the table. As quick as she is to shut the conversation down, I have a feeling New York has something to do with the part of the business Miles and his parents haven't been seeing eye to eye on.

Miles and I help with dishes and then say our goodbyes. Granny and Pops tell me I'm welcome anytime, and Mitch and Krista make it clear we better be over for dinner sometime this week so they can see us before they leave for Chicago to welcome their new grandbaby.

His family waits on the porch waving goodbye, but halfway to the truck, Miles stops.

"Hey guys, we're gonna go for a little walk. We won't be long, but we gotta work off that apple pie," he says, patting his ripped stomach like he's grown a belly from one meal.

"You kids take your time," Pops says while everyone else goes inside.

"Everything okay?"

"With you here, it sure is," he says distracted.

We walk around the house and back through the grass down to the dock. There is only a hint of the sun still painting the night sky. The lights bordering the property and lining the dock dance off the water, celebrating the arrival of tonight's nearly full moon.

It's magical.

If only the West Coast had lightning bugs like we do back East.

Talk about a fairy tale.

In all my time imagining the EBC logo coming to life, I never thought to imagine it at night. I know without a doubt I'll be adding an evening scene on a dock to my writing.

With the crickets and toads serenading us in the background, he sits in the chair on the right and pulls me down on his lap. He's got something on his mind, but I don't ask because I know he'll tell me when he's ready.

For now, I cuddle into him, letting him sit with his thoughts while I gaze at the dazzling lake in front of me and take in the last moments of light and the sounds of the evening.

"I'm thinking about taking EBC public."

He's sharing, but he's quiet, and I'm shocked at his statement.

"That's a big deal, Miles. Are you really just thinking about it or is it already in the works?"

"Well, I have interested investors."

"And?"

"And I really want to go international, and this would give us the capital to do that."

"How do your parents feel about it?"

"They're ready to retire. They think we should just sell and be done with it."

"Sell EBC?"

"I know, right?"

"If they have you to run things, why do they want to sell?"

"They think it's too much. They think I've been working too hard."

"I'd have to agree with them there, Miles."

"I know, but if we go public, we'll have a board, investors, shareholders. It won't be all on me. We can expand and have distribution centers all over the world and not just the US. EBC could be a global company. I could never have dreamed it was even a possibility. Even as it is now, things are way too successful for us to stay on top of. Even with the team in the Portland office, it's just too much. And we're growing so fast."

"Won't you lose a lot of control by going public?"

"Yes and no. I mean, I'll still be the president of the company, but decisions will have to go through the board."

"But EBC is your baby. You and your dad built it from the ground up. It's what you've dreamed of since high school."

"So, you don't think we should do it?"

"I didn't say that. I would just imagine it would be hard to give up control of your one true love."

"Mason, look at me."

I turn in his lap to look at him.

"I do love EBC. It's my family's business, and I love my family. But I only have one true love."

Gently pulling my face to his, he kisses me. Signifying, *I* am his one true love.

Sighing into his mouth, I say, "I love you too, Miles."

"I have some meetings with some possible investors coming up in New York in a couple of weeks, and I'd love it if you came with me. You could show me your town."

"I guess I do owe you a tour."

"Yes, you do."

"You sure I won't get in the way?"

"Nah, it's not like the meetings are gonna take all day and night, and there are only two. I'm just doing the right thing by meeting them in person, so they know we're not only serious but also appreciative of their interest in investing. The rest of my time would be all yours to do with as you please."

"Well, in that case, how can I say no?"

"Simple. You don't."

"Well, it sounds like we're going home for a few days. I'll let Katie know, and we can stay at my place."

"Brutal, you're gonna kick her out?"

"Seems we aren't the only two who have found love during our little house swap. Our sweet little Katie met someone, and apparently, they're official. She spends half her time at his place anyway."

"Good for Katie. If she's even half as happy as I've been since you walked into our little town, then she won't care where she's sleeping as long as it's with him."

"Um, so...I have a bit of news."

He pulls as apart so he can see my face.

"What's that?"

"I typed *the end* on book one yesterday."

"What? Yesterday? Why didn't you say something?"

"I don't know. I haven't ever had anyone to share that with except for the girls and the people paying me to write. I usually keep it to myself for a few days before I share."

"Well, thank you for telling me. When do I get to read it?"

I jump off his lap like he's on fire. "What?"

"You heard me. When do I get to read it?"

"Miles, I haven't even sent it to my editor yet. It's just the first draft. It's not perfect yet."

"I don't need perfect. But I do need to read this book inspired by our dreamy little small town."

He winks because what he really means is inspired by him.

"Well, the truth is, I was done, but now that I've been to Elsie Lake, I think I need to go fit in another chapter because I've just been inspired."

"How about this? Add your chapter and do whatever tweaking you want to do. As long as it is in my hands before we board the plane for New York, I can read it on the plane! Now, that sounds perfect."

"So, you want to be my beta reader?"

"If it means I get to read it first, then yes! Sign me up!"

"You sure?"

"I am. Now, sit back down and give me some more sugar."

CHAPTER 25

Miles

"Andy, this is Miles Montgomery," Mason says, introducing me to her salt and peppered doorman after greeting him with a hug.

Up close, he's much younger looking than I expected. Pretty fit too. The film industry sure has got it all wrong if handsome dudes who look like Andy are the norm.

"Nice to meet you, Mr. Montgomery," he says, extending his hand.

"Please, call me Miles."

And please keep your hands off my girl.

"Have you been taking good care of Katie these past two months?"

"Been doing my best, but since she found herself that new boyfriend of hers, I don't see her quite as often as I used to."

"I heard about him. He sounds like a good guy, but what's

your first impression? You're always a good litmus test on people."

"I do see a lot here from my front row seat, Miss Mason, that I do. So far so good with this guy. He's in the arts like her, so it could be a match made in heaven or…he could be like all the rest, but from what I've seen so far, he's a good guy."

"Well, that's good to hear and here's hoping for that match made in heaven."

I wrap my arm around Mason's waist and pull her close so her arm goes around me as a new possessive side of me that made its first appearance at the Let 'Er Buck Room at the Round Up this past week roars its ugly head again.

Last week it was due to close quarters and drunk cowboys and was perfectly acceptable. Today is more about making my place at Mason's side clear. Andy needs to know my role in her life. No need for him to make any assumptions when it comes to us.

"Well, we're gonna head up now. Miles will be staying with me and please let him in and out at any time. My place is his place, okay?"

"Of course, Miss Mason. Looks like your time in Oregon has been good for you. You look very happy."

"Damn straight, it's been good for her. And the best thing that's ever happened to me."

She turns into my chest and wraps both arms around me and locks her lips with mine in front of our audience of one.

You see that, Andy? Everything clear, buddy? I belong to her.

"I'm very happy. Thanks for noticing, Andy," she says to the attractive doorman, but still wrapped in my arms, she says the words to me as our eyes connect and our souls dance around the sound of the crackle in the air.

"Shall I bring your bags up for you?"

"Nah, I have it, Andy."

I can take care of her without your help, Mr. Doorman. Your services are no longer needed on that front.

Grabbing our bags, we catch the next elevator, and Mason holds a key fob up to the panel of buttons and then presses the one marked PH.

She stands with her hands in front of her instead of holding mine or touching me like she usually does.

She's nervous.

"Andy seems nice?"

"He's the eyes and ears of this place. Nothing goes on without him knowing about it. As a single woman, it feels good to have him there, and to know that he'll notice if something out of the norm is going on. He knows that no matter what they say, my parents and Grant are not allowed up without him calling me first. Those visits rarely if ever happen, but he has instructions for if they do. The poor guy has had to lie for me on more than one occasion."

Okay, I like the sound of that. I guess it's good he's there, and as long as he knows I'm the new man in Mason's life, then we're all good.

"Well, I'm glad you've had him in the past, but now you have me. I won't let anything bad happen to you, City Mouse."

Smiling, she says, "I'm glad you're here."

The elevator pings, and the doors open up to a small vestibule with a large door to the left. There is a small table with a vase of flowers next to the door where Mason sets her purse while she digs through it in search of her key.

"Found it," she says to the door as she turns the key.

Opening the door wide, she holds it for me as I carry our bags in.

"Home sweet home." She sounds a little unsteady.

She joins me on the edge of the huge all white and gray living room lined with floor-to-ceiling windows and a view of Central Park.

Holy shit.

"Wow, Mase. You weren't kidding." Leaving the bags in the entryway, I'm drawn to the huge windows and the vastness of the city spread out in front of us. "Baby, this place is off the charts. I see why you don't want to give it up. Can't say that I blame you." When I turn to face her, she seems startled, and I'm thinking I shouldn't have brought up the dreaded topic of her coming back to NYC so soon. "You should be really proud."

She's wringing her hands in front of her. Very un-Mason like.

"Can my city mouse not take a compliment?"

"I can," she says practically under her breath. "It's just strange to see you standing here in the middle of my world."

"Haven't you figured it out yet, Mase?"

She tilts her head confused.

"Your world is my world, and my world is your world, baby."

Standing there in her tight as hell skinny jeans, hot pink heels, and not-too-tight but tight enough white T-shirt strategically tucked in only the front, she's looking like she needs to be taken right then and there as she beams her light at me with her sexy as hell smile that tells me I've said exactly what she needed to hear.

"I like this look on you."

She looks down at herself as if she has no clue what I'm talking about. "What, jeans and a T-shirt?"

"Sweetheart, I think you know how good you look, and I think you know exactly what you were doing when you put it on this morning. I've had a semi all day."

"Miles…"

"Just say thank you for the compliment."

"Thank you. Want a tour?"

"If there is a bedroom somewhere on the tour, then lead the way."

"You have a one-track mind, Miles Montgomery."

"Mason, when it comes to you, there are so many tracks running through this brain of mine, you don't even want to know. Now show me your place and then I'm making love to you. Before we leave New York, I'm making sure we christen each and every room in the place."

"Luckily, it's only a two bedroom then. Otherwise, I'd never get a chance to show you my town."

"Oh honey, we aren't keeping this to the bedroom. I'm gonna have you up against that window before the day is done."

"Did I not mention I'm afraid of heights?"

"Then why live on the top floor of a sky-rise with floor-to-ceiling windows?"

She shrugs.

Walking toward her, she looks leery of me. She should be.

"You're scaring me, Miles."

She knows me well enough to know what's coming when I approach her this way.

Slow and steady.

"Be afraid, Mason. Be very afraid."

She kicks her shoes off, and before she's taken her second step, my arm is around her waist, preventing her escape.

"Where do you think you're going?"

"Miles! What are you up to?" She giggles while she struggles to get away from me, wanting a fun little game of cat and mouse.

"Baby, you know I love foreplay. I can play this little game of struggle snuggle as long as you want, but you know this is gonna end with you screaming my name, begging for more, and ultimately, with a big ole smile on your face, but if this is how you want to play it, we'll play."

I let her wiggle out of my arms, and she squeals as she runs into the kitchen, placing herself on the far side of the island. We've played the 'chase me around the island' game at my place. I always win.

She's breathing heavily, more from the anticipation and lust than any real physical exertion, her chest heaving with each breath. I love this playful side of hers. It feels good to know she can let loose and be silly around me. Show me all her colors.

Casually strolling around the island with my hands in my pockets, I see her eyes dart to the left and know when she's going to make her move. I let her take her first couple of steps and then before she has a chance to get too far, she's back in my arms. As soon as our bodies connect and that crackle fills the air, I'm done playing.

Swinging her legs up, I cradle her in my arms and march back into the living room.

Gently yet still playfully, I toss her on the gray overstuffed couch. She lets out another little squeal, but her playfulness is quickly being replaced with lust. She knows where this is going, and she wants it just as badly as I do.

I straddle her on the couch, my body engulfing hers and my lips devouring her like a dessert I can never get enough of. Never wanting the taste of her sweetness to end.

"Baby, what do you say we conquer that fear of yours?"

"Now?"

"No time like the present. Stand up for me."

Rising to my feet, I take her hand and help her up.

"Take it all off, baby."

"Miles…"

"All off."

This time, she doesn't question me and unzips her pants. While she's busy following my instructions, I go pick up her heels from the entryway and then bring them back and set them in front of her, earning a sexy smile from her lips.

I remove my shoes and socks, kick off my pants, and when I pull my shirt over my head, I'm met with the sight of my girl with only her lace panties on. I'm so hard for her I instinctually squeeze myself to try to ease some of the throbbing. When she shimmies out of the scrap of lace and steps into her hot pink heels, I growl with need but stop myself from tasting her.

Taking her hand in mine, I walk her to the window and feel her hesitance the closer we get.

"I got you. Now, come here and press that fine ass of yours up against the glass."

"Miles, you have got to be kidding me."

"Just look at me, Mase. Don't look down just look at me."

Never taking her eyes off mine, she turns her back to the window and steps backward until she's against the glass.

"Shit, that's cold."

"We're about to steam that shit up, so don't you worry. You won't be cold for long."

Letting go of her hands, I finish undressing and take a couple of steps back to admire her. She watches me watching her, and subtly, her legs close as she tries to fend off the throbbing she seems to be feeling too.

I've never seen anything like her. She is the most beautiful creature I have ever laid my eyes on, and sometimes when I see her like this—bared to me, vulnerable, and trusting me with her body—it overwhelms me.

Closing the distance between us, I get as close as I can without touching her except to take her hands in mine so I can put them above her head and hold her in place. "Mason O'Brien, you take my breath away and give me life all at once." Her big doe eyes fill with tears as my body presses against hers. "I had no idea how empty my life was before I met you. Or what it was like to love someone and have them love you back. To trust me to help take away their fears. You complete every piece of me. Nothing has ever fulfilled me the way you do."

She begins to speak, but I take her nipple in my mouth, effectively cutting her off.

"That's what you're doing right now by trusting me. You're fulfilling me. Body and soul."

I gently ease into her, and even though the view behind me is one many dream of, there is no way I'm taking my eyes off the woman trusting me with her soul.

"I love you, Mason. I love you so much."

CHAPTER 26

Mason

"It's so good to have you home and on a Thursday, no less!" Arianna, my adorable publicist, exclaims from the other side of the table.

She may be a petite little thing, but she's as tough and fiery as they come. When it comes to her friends and her job, she doesn't play. Always the sweetest person in the room until she's not.

"I'm so glad to be home, but you guys, Oregon is really great. And I can't wait for you to meet Miles. You're gonna love him."

"We better if we're letting him infiltrate Thursday night girls' night."

Keeping it real is Jackie, one of the copywriters I met during my time in the publishing world. She's fabulous and beautiful, loud and honest. She isn't from the Upper East Side, but you wouldn't know it by the way she owns her place in the city.

"Billie will be here shortly. She had a late shoot and is coming from set...well, speak of the devil, here she is."

Face wiped clean and hair up on top of her head, casual in leggings, Birkenstocks, and an oversized sweater, she is perfection as always. I pop out of my seat to squeeze the cover model.

"You're home, and you're in love! I want to hear every dirty detail!" she squeals, not wasting a moment.

The four of us take our seats, and for the next hour, I recount the past couple of months in Eastlyn. Starting with my first night at The Verdict all the way through today and our walk through Central Park. It's like one long verbal journal entry, only they ask questions and sigh in all the right places. I don't tell them all the dirty details, but I share enough. It's clear things are hot and heavy between the two of us.

"Now, he's determined to christen every room in my place, and so far, we're right on track to get it done in the next two days."

"Holy shit," Arianna says, looking as though she's seen a ghost.

"Sweetie, what's wrong?" I ask, turning to look over my shoulder as she shouts at me not to.

It takes me a few seconds to get past the shock of seeing my past and my future colliding. But once I do, I can't shake the confusion of what's in front of me.

Why?

How is this happening?

"Baby, there you are!" Miles shouts over the noisy restaurant.

"Miles…I don't understand? What are you…? What's going on?"

"Sorry, Mase. I know it's girls' night, and I shouldn't have brought a friend, but Mr. Kennedy and I hit it off and I wanted you two to meet."

"What do you mean your friend?"

"Aw, come on now, Mason, don't be that way."

Grant puts his arm around Miles, his hand landing on his shoulder, and Miles does the same. The sight is disturbing on so many levels. Please tell me Miles doesn't know who he is because

I'm not sure I could handle another betrayal of this kind of magnitude.

"Grant, why are you here?"

"No, honey, his name is Leland."

"Correct, Leland Grant Kennedy."

Grant has a sickening smile on his face, one I've seen on more than one occasion.

I can feel the bile rising in my throat, and before I know what's happening I'm fleeing the table and praying I make it to the bathroom in time.

I hear Billie hot on my heels the entire way, and she takes up the role of security guard outside the bathroom stall I find refuge in. But much to my surprise, nothing happens. Maybe getting the vision of the two of them with their arms around each other out of my head was all I needed.

"You okay in there?"

Pushing the stall door open, Billie is waiting for me with open arms.

Hugging me, she says, "So, Miles is cute."

We both giggle, but it's short lived.

"Billie, how could Miles bring him here? Did they already know each other? Have I been played?"

"I don't know, sweetie."

The door slams open, and Arianna looks like she's in need of a paper bag or she might hyperventilate. "Are you okay?"

"I'm fine, are you?"

"You better get out here, Mason. Miles put two and two together, and I have a bad feeling."

She turns rushing back to the table. Billie and I are right behind her.

Only the table is empty when we get there except for a shell-shocked Jackie. Past the table, I see the back of Miles and Grant as they press through the door and onto the sidewalk.

"Guys, what in the world is going on? I am so confused," Jackie asks from her chair.

Ignoring her question, I rush for the exit.

When we get to the street things seem calm. Grant is leaning against the building, and Miles is standing on the curb, keeping his distance. Relief washes over me until I hear their conversation and realize things aren't as civil as they appear.

"Listen, your little girlfriend fucked me over and wasted five years of my life."

This pisses Miles off, and he's no longer standing on the curb.

"So you thought you would fuck with her by fucking with me?" Miles says nose to nose with the asshole *I* wasted years of *my* life with.

Grant smirks. "Nah, seemed like a sound investment, to tell you the truth. Getting to see her face when we walked in together was just the cherry on top."

Comments like these from Grant are to be expected, but I've never witnessed the rage on the face of my sweet Miles. I should probably intervene before Miles ends up in jail.

Stepping between them, I address the one person I hoped I'd never have to see again.

"Grant, how did you even know we were together, and why do you care?"

Both men look at me, but Miles doesn't back away from him.

Unfazed, Grant answers. "Your mom follows all your Eve Villanelle social media bullshit."

"What does my mom have to do with you and your investments?"

"Oh, that's right, I got your parents when your stupid ass left me. God, you really are a selfish bitch."

I feel Miles leap forward, trying to go around me to get to Grant, so I turn to face him and push him back.

"Call her a bitch again! I fucking dare you!" he yells over my head, pointing at the asshole from my past who apparently has decided he needs to mess with my present as well.

Now, there are people watching through the restaurant window and the façade of civility is long gone.

"Miles, he isn't worth it. Just stop." I lift on my tiptoes to try to catch his eye, but he won't look at me. "I've heard it all before. I really don't care what he calls me."

Miles turns away from me on the sidewalk, but only makes it two steps before he turns back in my direction, finally looking me in the eye. He stares at me for a long beat, and when he believes that I really am okay, he settles in next to me, and we face Grant standing side by side, hand in hand.

"So tell me what in the world does this have to do with my parents?"

"You haven't heard then? Really?"

"Heard what, asshole?" Miles chimes in pulling me into his side.

"Just the fact that her dear old dad and I went into business together. He's my silent partner in LGK Inc. Turns out, I didn't need to marry her boring porn-writing ass to get what I wanted after all."

All the blood in my body rushes to my head, and it feels like I'm in a fog.

"Hey, she doesn't write porn!" I barely hear Billie yell from behind us.

"And she is far from boring!" Arianna chimes in, but it sounds like she's a million miles away and not two feet behind me.

"My dad knew about this?" I ask under my breath.

"What's that, baby? I can't hear you," Miles says.

"My dad knew you were meeting with Miles today?" I try again, finding my voice and praying I sound calm when, in reality, what tiny bit of my heart that still belonged to my parents is crumbling.

Miles squeezes my hand when he hears the sadness I clearly wasn't able to hide from at least him.

Grant just smiles like he's just won some unknown contest, but my farm boy isn't done.

"Well, you can tell Mr. O'Brien, not in this lifetime. I wouldn't let either of you pricks anywhere near my board or my company."

"Mason, you've really picked a winner, haven't you? I'm sure your dad is really going to love to hear how your new boyfriend called him a prick before they've even had a chance to meet."

Before I can comment, Miles ends the conversation.

"If her parents chose you over her, then they don't deserve my respect, and I'd happily tell them that face to face."

"And how do you feel about that, Mason?" Grant addresses me again.

This time, I get to say my piece.

I'm not sure if it's having the support of Miles and the girls behind me, or if it's from spending time with everyone I've met in Eastlyn, but I simply don't care anymore. I thought I was over losing what little relationship I had with my parents, but I realize until this moment that hadn't been true.

"You know what, Grant? You can have them. My well-being means as much to my parents as it did to you. They don't love me. They loved what having a daughter might have done for them, but it looks like you made all their dreams come true without me. And now that I think about it, the three of you were meant to be family. I know this because one of the most important things I've learned since I've been gone is that family is where you find it. You don't need the same blood coursing through your veins. When you meet people who matter to you, you get to choose. I'm choosing my family, and it's not you, and unfortunately, it's not my parents."

"Yes! You hear that, Grant? You don't matter!" Jackie yells from behind me.

Turning away from my past, I find Miles, my future, beaming down at me. Is it with pride, because I fought back? Joy that I alluded to choosing him to be my family? I'm not sure what emotion it is, but it feels good to be on the receiving end.

"I love you so damn much," Miles says through his gleaming smile.

"Still? Even after all of this?"

"Babe, like you just said, I choose you. You are my family, City Mouse."

I don't mean to start crying, but God, he always says the right thing, and right when I need him to say it.

I hear one of the girls sigh. "Oh, my God. They're perfect together."

Miles smiles. "Hell yes, we are." He kisses me quickly before addressing my friends.

"Ladies, I'm Miles, and it's nice to meet you. What do you say we head back in and get to know each other?"

I can't help but look over my shoulder as Miles walks us all back into the restaurant for one last look at my past, and I'm so glad I do. Grant is standing on the edge of the sidewalk hailing a cab, and when the yellow car pulls up, it drives right through a disgusting sewer water puddle that drenches his expensive suit and leaves me with one last perfect memory of him.

* * *

"Let me get this straight." Jackie leans over her third vodka cranberry, her eyes going back and forth between Miles and me, not believing what she's hearing. "Your opening line was, I'm. Going. To. Marry. You. One. Day."

"Yes, ma'am."

When she catches my ear-to-ear grin, her face that was screaming *what the hell* when she was looking at Miles metamorphosizes into *I'm so happy for you.*

"And you had only seen her from across the room? Hadn't spoken a word yet?"

"Yes, ma'am."

"Whoa." Billie sighs in awe.

Arianna continues to question him, and it doesn't faze him in the least.

"Ballsy. You use that one often?" Arianna asks, impressed.

"Never. But when you know, you know."

And because I've had a few cocktails myself, I share something I wonder if I should have the moment the words come out of my mouth.

"He calls it the *crackle*."

My knee is bumped by his under the table, and I'm pretty sure I shouldn't have shared.

"I'm sorry, what?"

"I was just…" I start to take it back and tell them I was just joking, but as I have learned about Miles, he doesn't shy away from his feelings, and he has no problem sharing.

"You know that feeling you get when the atmosphere in the room changes the moment your person enters? You feel them before you see them. Like there's some sort of crackle in the air." All three of them stare at him like he's speaking a different language. "You're telling me none of you have ever felt it before?"

Crickets.

My friends are taken aback, and these feisty New Yorkers, who are never short on words, are having trouble coming up with any.

"I think you've bewitched them with your too good to be true farm boy charm."

He kisses the corner of my mouth. "All that matters is that I've done the same to you."

"You sure have."

"And I'll do whatever it takes to make you stay under my spell until the end of my days."

"Okay, yep. I get it. Just felt it. The crackle is real, and you two have it." Jackie holds her phone up and takes a picture of us. "Sorry, just need a picture of what the crackle looks like."

"Babe, make sure you give her my number so she can send that to me."

"You have got to be kidding. You have more selfies of us and pictures of me to fill your phone to max capacity. The last thing you need is another picture."

"No worries. Jackie, make sure I give you my number before we go."

"You are ridiculous. I mean, really, what are you going to do with all of those pictures? You don't do social media. I seriously doubt you're going to have them printed and put in a photo album."

"You don't know everything, City Mouse. I may just surprise you," he says, lifting my hand and kissing the back of it.

"Speaking of knowing everything or each other really. I mean, how much time could you really have spent together in the past couple of months when you're running your company?" Arianna asks, always the pragmatic one.

And again, before I can speak, he does.

"Well, luckily for me, I have an assistant who kicks ass and takes names. I have a great team working for me, and for a couple of weeks during the harvest and my wooing my little City Mouse here, they were really picking up the slack. Things have gotten back to normal, and I'm doing the old nine to five while this one writes all day long. Also, it helps to be the boss. Means I can work when and where I want. It also means I work all day and night. There have been many nights I've been on my phone or my laptop while we're watching a movie or…"

Interrupting, I make sure the girls know that no matter what when we are eating dinner, or any meal for that matter, no electronics. No interruptions. I also clarify that his after hours working isn't that bad, and that I am always writing anyway, so it all works out.

"So, really it's like any couple. We work and see each other every night and on the weekends. Thank God, I can bust out of the office when I get the urge to see her. I mean, who's gonna fire me?"

"True, but how well do you really know her?" Billie leans in conspiratorially, whispering like I can't hear her. "I mean, your little city mouse has some serious issues."

"Is that so? Do tell, Billie. I'd love to hear this." I kid, knowing she would never sell me out for real but also knowing I have nothing to hide from Miles, and I'm fine with whatever she tells him.

"Well, for starters, she lives in a penthouse while being deathly afraid of heights. I mean, what's that about? Why live on the top of a high-rise if you're too scared to stand next to your windows and enjoy the view you spent all your hard-earned money on?"

"I did know that, but I do believe she's overcoming her fear. At least from the safety of her own home." We look at each other, the crackle between us loud enough for the whole place to hear. "You're rather fond of the view from your windows lately, aren't you, Mase?"

"No, you didn't!" Jackie yells. "You did her up against the windows of her apartment! Mason, I'm so proud of you!"

"Eww…stop it. I don't need to imagine that. Stop it. Stop it. Stop it."

"Arianna, don't pretend to be a prude just because there's a boy at girls' night," Jackie says, calling her out since she is usually the biggest perv of the group.

"But they're sitting right there. It's bad enough that I'm going to picture them naked up against those windows every time I'm there. You guys suck."

"If you ask me, this is the best girls' night ever!" Billie squeals.

"Okay, well, let's take your mind off it then. How else can I earn your faith in our relationship because I'm not going anywhere?" Miles asks the girls.

"Are you going to take her away from us?" Arianna cuts to the chase.

This is where I step in.

"Hey, that's a pretty serious question, and I don't think it's one we need to talk about tonight. Let's just say Miles and I are living in the moment and have decided we aren't talking about what happens when my house swap is over until the time is here. We're happy in the here and now, and that's all that matters."

The girls grow quiet, and I see the creeping doubt wash over them as they think about what I've just said. It sounds like we don't think this is going anywhere after my time in Eastlyn is over, but the truth of the matter is, we haven't talked about it since we got serious, and I am not about to have that conversation here with my friends in a crowded bar.

Even if it is on my mind twenty-four seven.

"I will tell you this, Arianna. No matter where things go…" Miles rolls his eyes as he says the words because in his mind, he knows where this goes. With me walking down an aisle in a white dress with him waiting at the other end for me. "I could never take you girls away from Mason. She loves you, you're her family, and you make her happy. From what I've gathered, this is sort of a package deal, and you guys are a little bonus to the big prize in the package."

God, I love this man.

"Mason, is he always this perfect?"

"Annoyingly, yes," I answer Jackie.

"Please tell me you have a single brother?"

"Sorry, just one happily married sister."

"Damn."

"You are sweet, kind, hot as hell, and let's not forget loaded since you essentially are EBC beer. So, except for the fact that you live in the middle of nowhere on the other side of the country, you're the complete package. It's too bad the only negative thing about you is so damn big because you're kind of perfect."

"Nah, I'm far from it."

The mood at the table grows a little somber at Arianna's comment. It's grounded in truth, and that's what makes it so hard to take.

Miles does what he does and lightens the mood and has everyone laughing until they cry, including me. Although under the surface, the 2700 miles between Eastlyn and New York City never leave my thoughts.

By the end of the evening, he has decided which of my girls are the Rachel, Emmett, and Amelia of my group. He tells them all about The Crew back home, and by the time the night is over, a trip to Eastlyn is in the works. Especially since we just told them that Emmett and I have been talking about opening a little new and used bookstore on Main Street. It's kind of shocking it doesn't already exist. I've been treating it like an investment, but I know it's really because I don't want to leave, and it's a reason to stay.

All this talk of Eastlyn has me missing it already, and we've only been gone two days.

What the hell am I going to do?

CHAPTER 27

Mason

Dear Journal,

IT'S *our third day back home, and we leave for the airport in six hours, but I don't see any sleep happening for me.*

To say these past few days have been a whirlwind of emotions would be an understatement.

Showing Miles my hometown, introducing him to my friends and having a run-in with my ex, who was trying to screw over the man I love, was already a lot. And as if all of this along with wondering what's going to happen when the next few weeks are over wasn't enough... there's more.

My mom.

She messaged me and said a lot of things. Unexpected things. And I don't know what to do with it.

I know, it's a lot, Journal.

It's been three years.

What did she say you ask?

Well, in a nutshell, she said she heard about what happened with Grant, and she was happy to hear what kind of man Miles was. She didn't like his name-calling but understood it. She said she's been watching my page and was glad to see me looking so happy and hoped I was getting the inspiration I was looking for in Eastlyn.

I was blown away by her words but never as much as I was with her last statement. She said she was sorry for the way things went with Grant, and she's glad things turned out the way they did, and that if all goes well, I'll spend my life with a man who not only loves me but is loyal and treats me like a princess.

Because. I. Deserve. It.

YES!!!!

She said that.

My mother.

No, I haven't written her back. I have no idea what to say. All I can think of is thank you.

When I told Miles, he just smiled and pulled me into his arms and didn't let go until I pulled away. He didn't try to say the right thing or tell me what to do. He just held me and left me with my thoughts.

My thoughts haven't stopped and are still going a million miles an hour.

A part of me is appreciative for her message, but another part of me is also leery and wondering when the other shoe is going to drop. After all, this is the woman who had the nanny read me my bedtime stories and was also the same woman who took Grant's side when we broke up.

I know I'm a grown woman in my thirties, but she's still my mom and somewhat of a mystery to me.

I'll reply eventually, but I'm not really ready to risk all the good I've been feeling lately when she is so good at making me feel the exact opposite.

I think I'll let it sit for a bit.

On another note...

Miles read most of the book on the way here, and he's going to finish it on the ride home. He refuses to discuss it with me and insists on a book club date. He's preparing his talking points as he goes, and when we get home, we have a date night planned to discuss his thoughts.

He couldn't be sweeter, and I love that he's doing this for me, but it's killing me not to hear what he thinks or talk to him about it. I may not sleep until date night.

CHAPTER 28

Miles

Dave clears his throat from the doorway, forcing me to peel my eyes from my computer for the first time in hours. Who knew brewing beer would turn me into a desk jockey? Not exactly what I had planned, but it's worth it. Right?

The look on his face erases the spreadsheets from my mind. Something's wrong.

"Hey, man, what's up?" I say standing and walking around my desk.

"Dude, I hate to be the one to tell you this, but Mel passed in his sleep last night."

"Mel? Our Mel?"

Not Mel.

Not the man I've seen every three weeks like clockwork since I was a toddler.

"I know, man, it fucking sucks. Margie found him this morning when she woke up."

Losing the strength to hold myself up, I sit in one of the leather chairs in front of my desk. Dave takes the one on my left, and we sit for a few minutes taking in the news.

Feeling helpless, I do the only thing I can think to do. Walking out into the hallway, I ask Bennett to come into my office.

"Okay, Bennett, we need to call George at the funeral home and tell him I have everything covered. No cutting corners. Whatever Margie and the family want. Then we need to call Mrs. Thoms and order every flower she's got. If there's any debt on the shop, I'll clear it. It's not like Mel had a 401k for Margie to cash in. We need to be sure she's taken care of."

"Got it, Boss. I'm on it."

"Everything!" I yell behind him. "I have it all covered. The family will not spend a dime, got it!"

"Understood!" he yells from down the hall.

Dave and I sit in silence again.

Still letting it sink in.

What is Eastlyn without Mel?

He's an institution.

My cell phone vibrates on my desk, and when I stand to check it, I see a text from Mason.

CITY MOUSE: Hey baby. Wanted to check on you. Did you hear the news about Mel?

ME: Just found out.

IN AN INSTANT, her face is lighting up my screen.

"Hey, baby."

"Oh, Miles. I am so sorry. Are you okay? I know how much he meant to you."

"I'm okay, baby. Thanks for checking on me."
"What can I do?"
She's just like me. Her first instinct is to help.
"Mase, I have everything covered, but I do think I'm going to have to postpone book club if that's okay?"
I feel awful because I know her book is a big deal, but I want to give her the attention she deserves, and after this devastating news, I'm not sure I'll be up for it.
"Miles, of course. Don't give it another thought. I understand if you can't get together tonight. I'm sure you want to be with your friends and family. Just let me know what I can do and I'm there. "
"Babe, no. I want to be with you. Let me rephrase that… I need to be with you tonight, but I'm just not sure I'll be in the right frame of mind to discuss your amazing work, and I want to give you my full attention when we do."
How could she have possibly thought I wouldn't want to have her in my arms on a night like this? She says that she understands how deep I'm in with her, but sometimes, I wonder if she really does.
"Okay, I'm yours, you know that. Whatever you need."
"You. I need you right now. In fact, fuck the office. It will be here tomorrow. I'm gonna wrap things up and head to you right now. Care if we stay at my place tonight?"
"Not at all. In fact, how about I meet you at your place? I'll let Lou out, and we'll be waiting for you when you get there."
"Thank you."
"No thanks needed. I love you, Miles."
"Fuck, Mason. I love you too."

* * *

LYING on my bed with one arm and one leg wrapped around Lou is my sleeping beauty.

Lou, who always greets me when I come in the house, is wide-awake and looking at me as if asking me what was he supposed to do when she's all wrapped up in him like this.

I get it, buddy. I wouldn't get up to greet me if this was my other option.

After snapping a few pictures of her before waking her up, I cuddle up behind her, and she rolls over as soon as she feels me against her.

Giving her a key to my place was the single smartest thing I've ever done.

"Hey, baby. Good nap?"

"It was. You better watch out. Lou's a pretty good cuddler."

"Mase, I will never share you with another man, but Lou and I have already talked. We have an understanding."

"Do you now?"

"Sure do. But that's between a man and his dog. I'm afraid I can't share those details with you. Just know that he knows where the line is drawn, and he knows not to cross it."

"Okay, Mr. Montgomery. I will leave that between you and Lou."

Her fingers trace my jawline, and she cups my face. "How you doing, sweetheart?"

"Better now that I'm here with you."

CHAPTER 29

Mason

The Smith Family funeral home is standing room only today.

It seems Mel Brown was more than just the local barber to most of the town. As the man who cut the hair of all of the men in town from toddlers to the retired, he was as much of a therapist as he was a barber.

Every business on Main Street is closed for this afternoon's service. All of Eastlyn is in mourning.

As the new girl in town and for such a short period, I consider myself incredibly fortunate to have spent what limited time with him that I did. I was only in the shop once, but I get it. Mel's is a living, breathing museum, and he loved each and every person in this town. And that love was returned tenfold if the turnout today is any indication.

There have been deaths in my parents' circle of friends, and yes, there is a big turnout to those services as well, but they don't feel like this. There is no sense of community or real care for the loved ones who have lost someone dear to them. It all still feels like a business transaction. Everyone is there, so they don't miss an opportunity, and most of all because of how it looks. And if the O'Briens have one thing down, it's appearances.

Over this past week, Miles has been just as busy as ever with work. In addition to taking care of Margie and Mel's family, the arrangements for today, he made sure everyone knew that the shop was still open and trying to keep business flowing to his employees, Mac and Floyd.

This past week reminds me of what it must have been like during the blackout in Vegas. The first day I met Emmett and Amelia at the salon, and how they were talking about how Miles kept everyone calm and was the person in the group who took care of everyone. Just as he's doing now when the people of Eastlyn, especially when one family in particular, need him most.

If only more of his Crew family were here to support him. With Parker and Audrey all the way on the other side of the country, Rachel and Reece in Africa, and Emmet and Josh now all living out of town, it's only Miles and Amelia representing their handpicked little family of friends.

Through it all, he has spent more time with me during the week than usual. Not only have we spent all of our evenings together, but I've also hung out at the EBC office either writing or wandering about the brewery when he's on calls or in meetings. He's asked me to go with him to run errands, let Lou out, and do all things domestic with him. He's even had me go with him when he visited Mel's family. Watching him with them causes my love for him to run deeper and deeper.

He isn't putting on a show.

This is who he is.

All of his work this week to make sure today honored his friend in the right way was not for his gain.

He cares about them, and even in their time of sorrow, you

can see their appreciation for his generosity, even if he refuses to really acknowledge everything he's done for them.

This week has been the first time I have seen Miles treated as more than just the good old local boy who made a name for himself. When people see him in action like he has been, rallying the town together to take care of their own, they look at him like this is his town and they are his citizens. Like he's the King of Eastlyn. And with me at his side, I have unfairly been treated just as well. I have shook an unknown amount of hands and held babies. I've made phone calls and even a pie or two.

Friday night he even spoke during halftime at the high school football game. He helped the Eagles dedicate their season to Mel and spoke as though he were the school representative. It was touching and heartfelt, and my love for Miles and this town grew even stronger that night.

Through this tragedy has come a true blessing with the knowledge that I want to be here next to this man and with these people.

I haven't said it out loud, and I still have moments of uncertainty and fear. Not only about whether I would be willing to give up New York for Eastlyn but there is also the unknown of what Miles truly wants.

When he said we weren't going to talk about the end of my stay here, he meant it. He doesn't joke about marriage anymore, and every day is spent living in the moment.

There is no denying that the strength of our relationship grows every day, and he looks at me like the sun rises and sets in my eyes. But not talking about our next step has had me tied up in knots.

Sitting here in Smith's Funeral Home is one of those moments when I feel a bit out of place. I mean, what am I doing here? I've been here just over two months. I feel like an intruder.

But then Miles squeezes my hand before he releases it to go up and say a few words.

Standing behind the podium, he eloquently expresses his feelings and tells stories from his childhood involving Mel.

From his time in the shop to baseball games sponsored by that same shop. He highlighted his skills as a two-stepper and someone who made the best brisket in the county.

Those in attendance are laughing openly at a silly story involving Mel, a raccoon family, and a plate of steaks.

But those tears of laughter turn to those of sorrow when he changes the topic to love.

"If you knew Mel, you know that his world began and ended with Margie. He loved her something fierce, and his loving wife and children were his everything. Yes, it seemed he was always at the shop, but he was also at every game, recital, dinner, and bedtime story, and I don't think Mel and Margie have spent more than a night or two apart in their sixty plus years of marriage."

Miles grows quiet for a moment, his eyes finding mine and holding steady from across the room.

My heart is his.

No question.

"You know, it was just two weeks ago that I was last in Mel's' chair." He's speaking right to me. Telling me to listen carefully with his intent stare. "We were talking about love. Well, he was telling me that he could see that I had fallen pretty hard, and he remembered how it felt when he fell in love with Margie. In fact, his exact words were, 'I remember what it is to lose your reason over a woman, Miles. In fact, I lost all my reason the day I met Margie, and well, it's been over sixty years, and she never did give it back.'"

He turns his attention to Margie.

"You were his sun and moon. He loved you with his whole heart. And I know he's here by your side today. He'll always be here with all of us."

Miles steps down from the podium and stops in front of the

Brown family and quietly offers his condolences before joining me three rows behind them.

When he fills his spot next to me, he pulls me in tight against his side and kisses me on my temple.

For the rest of the service, I can only think one thing over and over.

Love.

Love.

Love.

Love.

I know we're here because of a great loss, and I feel that, but I also feel so much love for the man with his arm around me. My tears are seen to everyone around me as sorrow, only I know that they are also due to the overwhelming swelling of my heart.

And the strangest thing is I can't wait to tell my mom.

I wrote her back the night we got back to Eastlyn, and we've been messaging each other every day since.

I can't excuse decades of poor parenting, but I've decided to try to have some sort of relationship with her. Over the past week, she has not only acknowledged and apologized for her behavior, but I'm beginning to understand her a little better.

Because she had married who she had been told to marry and was raised to do as her husband told her, just as her mother had, she was only doing what she knew.

Last night, her message said she knew she had done it all wrong when she saw the first picture of Miles and me together on my page. She saw something in my eyes she had never seen before, and she knew it was happiness. She realized she kept that from me for most of my life, and she was grateful to get to see it even if only via pictures on social media.

I'm still treading lightly, but it's been nice to talk to her this way. I think not being face to face has helped, and we've both opened up more than we would have in person.

So, with the emotions coming from the heartbreak of Mel's

death, the communication with my mother, and all of the love hitting me square in the chest right here in this pew, I'm overwhelmed and silently bawling my eyes out.

I feel like a sponge being run dry.

We're all asked to stand as the family is the first to leave the room.

Miles takes my face in his hands, and whispers, "Hey, baby, you okay?"

I nod furiously.

"You sure."

I rise up on my toes and confess in his ear.

"I just love you so much. I can't imagine ever losing you like this. It's too much to even think about."

Wrapping his arms around me, he holds me tight until it's time for our row to exit. When he releases me, there are tears streaming down his face as well. Now, I'm the one holding his face in my hands. I wipe his tears with my thumbs, and we exit our row and walk hand in hand out of the funeral home.

CHAPTER 30

Miles

"So you hand delivered it? Like you put it in her hand?"

"Sure did," Bennett says, unable to hide his smile.

He can laugh at me all he wants.

I'm trying to woo a girl here.

"And she read it and told you she'd be there."

"Not only did she say she'd be there but she also asked if she could bring anything."

I chuckle. "Of course she did."

"She seemed pretty excited. Couldn't stop smiling."

That's my girl.

"Okay, so you have things here then?"

"Just as I always do."

"And unless the damn sky is falling, I don't want any interruptions of any kind tonight. None whatsoever. We're clear on that, right?"

"Crystal."

"Excellent."

I start looking all over my office unable to find…what, I have no idea.

"Keys?" Bennett questions.

"Shit. Yes, keys. Thank God my ass is attached or I'd lose that too. Thanks."

"That's what I'm here for."

"Thanks, man. I appreciate your help. I know it goes above the call of duty."

"No problem. I have everything here. You just have a good night, and I'll see you tomorrow!" he yells after me as I race out of the office, through the brewery, and out a side door to my truck.

I HOP IN THE TRUCK, but don't start the engine right away as I take a moment to look at the giant building in front of me. The accumulation of Dad's and my dream. It started with a teenager, his old man, and a dream.

Here we are.

We did it.

I didn't think I had anymore dreams to fulfill, but I couldn't have been more wrong.

There's a dream come to life right here in Eastlyn, and she leaves in less than a week.

Five days to be exact.

I'm not panicked.

I'm sure.

Sure of us.

Here goes nothing.

CHAPTER 31

Mason

You are cordially invited to an afternoon of Book Talk.

Please join me at:
The home of Miles and Lou Montgomery
2055 SE Lincoln
Eastlyn, OR

Time: 2:30 p.m.

Please R.S.V.P. to the gentleman standing in front of you upon receipt of this invitation.

*Complimentary wine, hors d'oeuvres, and German shepherd included.

Grabbing my invitation off the counter and taking a deep breath, I take one last look at myself in the mirror. The weather has changed dramatically in the past few days, and the gray sky looks moody, to say the least. I think rain is on its way, and so with the change in the weather comes a change to my wardrobe.

Staring back at me in light blue skinny jeans, an oversized khaki sweater hanging off one shoulder, and light brown ankle boots with her hair curled in perfect waves and wearing barely there makeup is a woman who looks scared to death.

And I am.

We're finally going to discuss the book. I am knowingly and willingly attending an event where my work is going to be judged and scrutinized by the man I love, and that scares the crap out of me.

What scares me even more is what happens five days from now when Katie comes home. He's made no mention of it, yet it's all I can think about.

"You got this, Mason," I say to the image in the mirror. "Unless he thinks your writing is crap and breaks up with you because of it, tonight you will discuss where this is going, and you will have a plan for what is to come once the house flip comes to an end. You are not leaving his place without having a real discussion."

Leaving the house fifteen minutes before the time on my invitation should have me there with about seven minutes to spare. I head out with my shoulders back, confidence in place, and doubt left behind.

Usually one to have music playing at all times in the car, I'm almost to his place before I realize the car is silent except for my own voice practicing what I want to say to Miles when I bring up our relationship and where we'll be this time next week.

As I pull up to his house, my fears change course and focus on the book talk about to take place. I'm more afraid to hear what Miles has to say than I have ever been with my editor.

But all is well when I see the sweet black and tan boy waiting for me in the front window. I do believe he's wearing a business tie.

What in the world?

Lou's smiling face calms my nerves. And I run from the car to the front door, looking up at the sky surprised it hasn't opened up just yet. I'm not mad the rain has stayed away, though. No need to look like a wet dog while we discuss my words.

More like my heart and soul poured on to the page. But no biggie. It's just a book, right?

Here goes nothing.

When I open the door and let myself in I'm met with not only a tie wearing German shepherd but also his studious looking father, well sort of. He's got on worn jeans, a light blue button-down shirt, backward EBC baseball cap and to top it off glasses.

Holy hotness!

"Well, if it isn't the guest of honor. We're honored to have the author of this month's book club selection here at our humble little book chat, aren't we, Lou?"

"You're crazy. What's with the glasses?"

Instead of answering my question, he kisses me long and hard, and I couldn't care less what he thinks about the book. As long as he kisses me like this, all is right in the world.

Much too soon, he releases me and walks me to the living room.

"What did you do?" I gasp, trying not to cry.

"Well, you sent me an eBook copy of the book, and that just won't do for a book club meeting, will it? Don't worry, we did it at the office, so it's all secure. Your words are not floating around out there for anyone to steal. Bennett and I did it ourselves."

In front of me, the table is adorned with a bottle of wine, two glasses, fruits, cheeses, crackers, and two printed copies of my book. On the cover page of each stack of pages it says:

The Book with No Name

Written by: City Mouse

"If you'd like to take your seat, we can get started."

I sit in my favorite spot on the couch. He covers me in a blanket and pours me a glass of wine.

It takes a minute before the blanket registers, but when it does, my heart skips a beat.

"Miles, what have you done?"

"Oh, you mean, what have I done with all the pictures you said were just filling up my phone and that I would never do anything with?"

"Miles, my face is everywhere."

"I know, isn't it great?"

"Miles..."

"Don't worry, I won't make you say you were wrong. Or that I'm a genius."

"I think genius maybe pushing it. When did you take all of these?"

The blanket on my lap is covered in pictures of me sleeping with Lou, taking pictures on the farm, sitting at the kitchen table writing, blow-drying my hair, blowing him kisses, posing with my girls in New York, and with his Crew at The Verdict. It's amazing and embarrassing all at once.

"Honey, I told you, you didn't know everything there is to know about me. I have to keep things interesting. This way even if you aren't here, I can still wrap you around me."

Even if I'm not here.

There it is.

"So I did a little research on book clubs and learned that sometimes attendees come dressed like their favorite characters, and I figured I had the outfit so I thought what the heck." Lifting the glasses up and down, he continues. "Picked up these bad boys at the pharmacy and bam! I'm Tucker Rhinehart! Hot sandy-haired farm boy who looks good in a pair of jeans and a backward baseball cap. Oh, and glasses."

"Interesting, I didn't see the similarities between the two of you until now. Must be the glasses." I giggle.

"Are the specs supposed to be my Clark Kent disguise?"

It's suddenly way too hot to be curled up in a blanket, but all I want to do is hide underneath it. But I promised myself I wouldn't let myself hide my feelings today, and I guess there's no time like the present to start.

"I had a pretty hot muse."

"Yes, you did." He bends down and kisses me quickly before taking a seat in the armchair across from me. "Shall we begin?"

"That's what we're here for."

I grab a pen and the journal I used to plot *The Book with No Name* out of my bag ready to take notes.

Lou lies down at his daddy's feet, and we both take a sip of wine. Miles picks up his printed copy of *The Book with No Name*, and my heart trips over itself.

"Chapter One..."

* * *

Two hours and thirty chapters later, we're finally to the end. Except for one small break that included strawberry shakes delivered from Tom's, we haven't gotten off track. I thought he may start off all formal and that the book club schtick would wear off at some point, but he was serious.

We've gone chapter by chapter and discussed the characters, the storyline, and oh yes, the sex scenes. He was particularly detailed with those sections. He also gave me some pretty productive notes. He pointed out a few spots where the hero's dialogue didn't really sound like something a guy like Tucker Rhinehart would say, which really meant Miles would never say it. He corrected my terminology when describing farm equipment and other little details that most readers wouldn't notice but were important to him to get right.

But most of all, he loved it. He talked about the characters like they were real people, and he couldn't believe so and so would say that or how could this character do that? It was incredibly endearing and warmed my topsy-turvy heart along the way.

He did have one major issue with the book, though.

"Mase, it just ends. What happens? Does she stay or go?"

"It's called a cliffhanger, Miles. This is book one of a four-book series. We can't wrap it all up in the first book."

"Well, I now know I don't like a cliffhanger. It's so unfair."

"You'll just have to wait for book two."

"As the leader of this here book club, shouldn't I get special privileges?"

"And what kind of privileges would that be?"

He finally leaves his chair that's felt so far away all the way over on the other side of the room and joins me on the couch. That was far too long with him so close but too far away to touch. Next to me is where he needs to be.

He scoots me down onto my back and hovers above me playfully pinning me into the spot.

"The kind of privileges where you tell me what happens."

"Where's the fun in that?"

I lean up to kiss him, but he pulls away.

"No sugar for you until you tell me what happens." He stands and offers me his hand, pulling me to my feet.

"Miles, you can't ask an author to give away the ending to their story."

"But I just did."

"Well, what if I don't know the ending yet?"

He wraps his arms around me. "You really don't know the ending yet?"

All I'm brave enough to do is shrug.

"Hmm…well, how about we go have a beer and see if we can figure out the ending and maybe even a name for the damn book."

"Don't you have beer here?"

"Sure do. But it tastes better when Beau pours it."

Very true.

* * *

Fifteen minutes later, our butts are on barstools and full pints of EBC are in our hands.

"Cheers to Katie for getting her gig on Broadway and sending you my way."

"Cheers to that, indeed."

We clank our glasses together and take our first sips.

"Here you got a little something right here…"

His tongue finishes his sentence licking the foam off my top lip while his lips write the rest of the paragraph, telling a story of lust, love and forever.

"Thought I wasn't going to get any sugar until I told you the ending to Tucker and Camille's story?"

"Baby, how could I not give in to you when we're here at the scene of the crime?"

"I don't believe I've committed any crimes, Mr. Montgomery."

He turns my stool so we're knee to knee and eye to eye.

"City Mouse, the night you walked into this bar, you stole my heart and still haven't given it back."

"You probably say that to all the girls you meet in this place."

"Nah, I usually start by telling them I'm going to marry them one day."

The sincerity in his eyes speaks volumes, and my stomach does somersaults at the thought that there may be more going on than just a beer at The Verdict.

And with impeccable timing, his phone vibrates on the bar, breaking the vulnerability of the moment. He reads his message, his leg bouncing up and down, and throws back the rest of his beer. When he takes a twenty out of his wallet and throws it down where his phone had been lying, I can't help but think something about his text message upset him.

"Hey, everything okay?"

"Yeah, everything's great, why?"

"Are we leaving?" I ask, tipping my head toward the money on the bar.

I see him notice that I haven't really put a dent in my beer yet and he relaxes a bit.

"Um, no...take your time. Whenever you're ready. We just need to head over to Granny's when we're done."

"Oh, well, you should have said something." I toss back my beer in one long chug. "Ready."

"You're a freaking unicorn, you know that?" he says in awe.

"Nah, just a fan of Granny and EBC. Shall we?"

We're halfway through the bar when one of the songs we danced to the night I agreed to come out with the girls comes on, and he redirects us to the dance floor.

"This is one of the best country songs ever recorded."

"We've danced to this before."

"Ah, so what you're saying is you've burned every moment we've spent together into your memory bank?"

He leans in close, and the warmth of his breath on the shell of my ear sends the good kind of shiver down my spine.

"Me too, baby."

We sway in time with the sweet song about a chair, but it's over much too soon, and then we're headed back in the direction of the exit sign.

It's dark now, and the moment Miles shuts the truck door, the dark skies finally open up and the rain showers down on us.

"Shit! You've got to be kidding me!"

"What's wrong?"

"Nothing."

"Okay?"

He sends a text before putting the truck in drive.

The ride to his grandparents' house is quiet. He's in his head somewhere or just really, really hates rain. Not sure which, but his mood has taken a slight turn, and I decide to give him his space while he works it out.

Before long, the gravel road that leads to Elsie Lake is under our tires, and he still seems a little stressed.

He parks the truck, and I start to open the door, but he stops me and says he'll be right back.

He runs into the house and is gone a couple of minutes before returning to the truck with an umbrella big enough for two.

"Miles, I could have run to the front door. You didn't have to get an umbrella. I won't melt."

"I know, but we aren't going in the house."

"We aren't?"

"Nope, I have a little surprise for you."

"For me?"

"Come on, let's go for a walk."

"A walk? Right now, Miles?"

"Baby, just work with me on this, please?"

Oh boy, so there's a reason he's pissed it's raining, and me fighting him on it is stressing him out even more. What in the world is he up to?

"Sure, honey."

We follow the path that takes us around the side of the house, and when we emerge in the backyard, the dock is lit up with hundreds of white lights. It's absolutely beautiful.

"Miles, what in the world is going on?"

"Just wanted to do something special for you. Wasn't expecting the rain, but we can work around it. Come on."

We follow the pathway to the dock, the lights, and at the end, of course, two weathered Adirondack chairs.

Just standing there huddled under an umbrella in the pouring rain, I finally ask, "Uh, Miles. What's going on?"

He nods his head in the direction of the house. "He should be able to fill you in."

Sweet Lou is running toward us, and once he's in front of us, Miles gives him a signal, and he sits.

"Miles, how in the world did he get here, and why is he out here in the rain too?"

"It looks like he has something for you."

Sure enough, something is hanging from his neck. I lean forward to take a piece of paper out of a zip lock bag that's been attached to his collar, and Miles follows me with the umbrella to keep me dry.

"What is this?"

"Well, I don't know. It's from Lou, not me. Why don't you read it and see what it says? Read it out loud, though."

The rain is drumming on the umbrella nearly as fast as the

thumping of my heart as I unfold the letter in my shaking hands.

"Out loud please," Miles reminds me.

"Mason, Dad and I love you more than kibble and beer. More than sunrises during harvest and bonfires at The Jumps. More than strawberry shakes and walks through Central Park. More than his old truck and more than my throw stick. If you're willing to put up with Dad for the rest of your life, we'd sure like to love you forever."

Barely able to see the words on the page through my tears, I turn to Miles, and he hands me the umbrella and steps out into the pounding rain and bends down onto one knee.

"Miles, get back under here, you're getting soaked!" I yell over the pounding rain.

"Baby, you can have my umbrella, my heart, my last breath. All of it. All of me. In fact, you already have all of that." He's yelling over the rain but pauses to pull a box out of his front pocket. "The only thing of mine that I haven't given you yet is my last name."

Speechless, I stare at him from the security of the umbrella while he pours his heart out in front of me in the rain. I can see the sparkle of the ring in the box he's holding up to me, but I couldn't tell you what it looks like because the sight of Miles soaked to the bone asking me to be his is more powerful than the shine any ring could ever project when competing with the love of my life.

"We'll split our time between here and New York. We'll have babies or we won't have babies. I just need to be your husband, Mason. That's really all there is to it. So how does it end, baby? Does she stay or does she go?"

Without thinking, I kneel on the wet dock holding the umbrella over both of us. He kneels on both knees with me and waits for my answer.

"She stays, Miles. She stays."

"She sure as hell does."

RAISED ON IT PLAYLIST

Ex To See (Acoustic Mixtape) by Sam Hunt
My Boo by Usher & Alicia Keys
Kinfolks by Sam Hunt
Get Me Some of That by Thomas Rhett
Small Town Boy by Dustin Lynch
Favorite T-Shirt by Jake Scott
The Chair – George Strait
A Simple Song by Chris Stapleton
The Daughters by Little Big Town
Homemade by Jake Owen
Raised On It (Acoustic Mixtape) by Sam Hunt
Make Me Wanna by Thomas Rhett
Cowboy Take Me Away by Dixie Chicks
That Old Truck by Thomas Rhett
Good Time by Niko Moon
Talk by Khalid
The Difference by Tyler Rich
If It Feels Good (Then It Must Be) by Leon Bridges
Girl, I Wanna Lay You Down by ALO featuring Jack Johnson
Electricity by Silk City, Dua Lipa, Diplo, & Mark Ronson

RAISED ON IT PLAYLIST

If We Never Met by John K
Details by Billy Currington
Things You Do For Love by Thomas Rhett
One Man Band by Old Dominion

Listen on Spotify

WHAT TO READ NEXT

The Between the Pines Series
(Meet *The Crew* from Eastlyn in this four book series of standalone contemporary romance novels.)

We Are Tonight
Raised On It
Bottle It Up – Preorder Now
Leave the Night On – Preorder Now

Blackbird
Standalone second chance contemporary romance.

The Gorgeous Duet
A steamy, suspenseful romance about breaking the rules and following your heart.

Gorgeous: Book One
Gorgeous: Book Two

The You & Me Series

Read this three-book series of sweet and sexy standalone novels filled with love, loss, secrets, and sass.

You & Me: Part One
You & Me: Part Two
More
Something Just Like This

ABOUT THE AUTHOR

Lisa Shelby is an ever-so hopeless romantic and self-professed love geek. Born and raised in the Pacific Northwest and proud to call Oregon home. It's here that she resides with her husband, son and two dogs dogs. Reading has been her obsession and writing had been her secret passion. It was that passion that led her on my journey to write a book for her husband. What began as a gift turned into an inspiration of love and the desire to share that love with everyone. With the encouragement of her husband and the support of her family and friends, she began her journey and published her debut novel, "You & Me" in September 2016 and hasn't stopped since.

Follow Lisa everywhere: @lisashelbybooks

Made in the USA
Columbia, SC
21 September 2020